Besieged

The Scottish Falconers
Book One

By Diane Wylie

Cover design: Sheri McGathy

Discover more about Diane Wylie at
http://www.dianewylie.com.

Dedication

To Ed, Scott, Elaine, Kurt, Ben, Kate, and my
whole family, who make my life sweet.
To my friends from long ago and my friends
from today, who make memories to treasure.

Author's Note

For the sake of the story, I have slightly changed the history regarding the smuggling of the Honours of Scotland from Dunnottar castle. The Graham family members are all fictional characters, and they did not actually take the royal artifacts out of Dunnottar. In my research, two accounts of this act exist. Either Christian Fletcher, the wife of the minister of Kinneff Parish Church, or Fletcher's servant carried the crown, sceptre, and sword out of the castle.

In addition, I gave the falcons more abilities than the normal trained peregrine falcons, as I don't believe they can be used to track people, and I am told they have no real loyalty to people.

The child in the story, William Ogilvie, was actually born later to Sir George Ogilvie's second wife, Margaret Arbuthnot, and not to Elizabeth Douglas.

I hope you agree that these minor tweaks in reality added to the entertainment value of the story.

Diane Wylie, Author

Praise for Diane Wylie's other titles…

"…You hate for this to end. A must read for paranormal readers and has made me a believer."

~P.E. Patterson, Amazon reviewer (about MAGIC OF THE PENTACLE)

"…I highly recommend this book to anyone who enjoys a good romance and mystery. The author did not leave you wanting."

~Linda Tonis, member of the Paranormal Romance Review Team (about MOONLIGHT AND ILLUSIONS)

"…as I read the story, I simply could not put it down until I had devoured every last word…"

~Rie McGaha from Romance Writers United (about LILA'S VOW)

"…an author who displays a rare talent and leaves you wanting more…"

~Marilyn Rondeau from RIO— Reviewers International Organization (about SECRETS AND SACRIFICES)

"…Ms. Wylie gives historical romance a breath of fresh air…"

~Sandra Marlow from Romance Junkies (about JENNY'S PASSION)

"…Wylie expertly brings the reader back in time as she weaves the perfect web of history, lust, and intrigue…"

~Jennifer Vido from Fresh Fiction (about SECRETS AND SACRIFICES)

Other Titles by Diane Wylie

Secrets and Sacrifices

Daughters of the Civil War series:
Book One — Jenny's Passion
Book Two — Lila's Vow

Adam's Treasure
A Soldier to Love
Outlaw Lover

Mark of the Magician series:
Prelude to Magic
Book One — Moonlight and Illusions
Book Two — Magic of the Pentacle
Book Three — Magic at the Roxy

Chapter 1

February 1652
Scotland

Catriona Dunn placed a crusty loaf of round bread into the basket of a waiting customer and caught the movement of something large out of the corner of her eye.

She turned her head, and her mouth dropped open at the sight. Riding past their bakery cart was the most beautiful sight she had ever seen. A most handsome, brown-haired young man sat astride a sleek black horse with a white blaze down its face. Sitting on some sort of perch attached to the saddle was a rather large gray bird. The bird had some sort of fancy cover on its head and could not see.

"Did you never see the Governor's falconers before?" her customer asked.

"N-no, mistress." Catriona's face went hot. "This is my first time inside the castle walls."

"Aye, and you're not wanting it tae be yer last, so you'll attend to business. Isn't that right, Cat?"

Catriona quickly accepted the woman's coins and turned to her father. "So sorry, Da, there's just so many interesting things to see."

"Like the dashing young Rabbie Graham, I suppose."

"Aye, it will do no harm to be looking."
With a placating smile, she dropped the coins
in her father's big apron pocket.

"Och, Cináed," the matronly woman
broke in, giving Catriona a wink, "ye ken
how ye like to oggle the pretty women
yerself. Ye can scarcely blame yer daughter.
She'll be needing a find young buck to
marry."

Heat rushed up from Catriona's belly to
her face. There had been no such idea in her
head. A husband was the last thing she
wanted right now.

As she glanced over at her big bear of a
father, the guilty look on his face told the tale.
The woman had been correct about her Da.
She mentally shrugged. So they were both
appreciative of a finely formed Scots. Only he
liked the females and she liked the males. For
a long time, Catriona had hoped her father
would remarry after her mother had died, but
he had not "found the right one."

"We need not be rushing m'girl. There'll
be time aplenty fer her to wed." With that,
Cináed winked at his daughter.

Catriona huffed. "I'll be wedding
whenever I've a mind tae, Da. "'Twill no be
on yer terms, 'twill be on mine … and his."

"And would you be setting yer sights on
winning young Rabbie Graham to woo ye?"
Her father enveloped her in a big, smelly hug,
his beefy arms nearly crushing the breath out
of her. "If I had such a braw son-in-law, we'd
be wanting fer nothing. His father is the
Grand Falconer, and his family serves Sir

Ogilvie, who treats them verra well for those birds."

"Want does he do with the birds, Da?" Catriona's voice was muffled behind his mass.

"Take a look for yerself, lass. Ye kin see them from here." Da released her and pointed to the right. They had a clear view of the open courtyard past the market. Two women held big birds, just like Rabbie's bird, on gloved hands, while three men, Rabbie included, put the birds through their paces.

The red-haired young man had a long, thin rope with a brown-colored object at the end. Catriona could not tell what the object was from where she stood watching. The man pulled the object along the ground as he ran backward. Someone whistled and the older woman moved her arm upward a bit. The bird she held took to the sky.

Long wings beat the air then the falcon dropped down on the object and gripped it with its claws.

Rabbie Graham approached the bird. Catriona's heart beat a little faster as she watched his smooth, fluid motions. He wore high, close-fitting brown leather boots that showed off muscular calves. A fashionably loose-fitting shirt hid the lines of his upper body, but tight breeches gave mute evidence of more muscles.

He extended his gloved right arm and whistled. The bird immediately left the ground, came to roost on the glove, and ate something from Rabbie's fingers.

An older man walked over, and the three men conversed for a moment. When the two women came up, Rabbie transferred the peregrine to the older woman's glove. She turned and walked away with her long skirt swirling around her legs.

The younger woman was dressed in breeches and boots like a man. This time, she let loose her bird while Rabbie ran and dragged the object for her bird to catch.

Catriona mused on how good Rabbie looked when he loped along, compared with the red-haired lad, who just looked silly.

For hours, she snuck peeks at the falconers while they worked and while she tended to her customers. The five people seemed so close-knit. Just then, Rabbie gave the red-haired young woman a big hug. Catriona's entire body went hot then cold.

Was that his wife? Her heart sank.

Chapter 2

As soon as she followed the donkey-pulled bakery cart past the vendors stocking their booths, Catriona craned her neck to find the Graham falconers. Every day since Da had allowed her to come with him to Dunnottar Castle, she had watched the family working with birds of all sizes and, apparently, all different stages in their skill level. Da had identified each person for her. It turned out that the red-haired girl was Rabbie's sister. Catriona was happy again.

How she wished Da would have allowed her to come to Dunnottar sooner, but since he had been set upon by thieves one night while he was on his way home, he hadn't wanted to risk the life of his only remaining family member, or so he said. Spending her days alone in their cottage had been both boring and, at times, frightening. Da said she should not allow her imagination to get away from her. The cottage and their separate bakehouse were well hidden in the woods and far from the place where he had been attacked.

It was true, though, she did have a vivid imagination. Sometimes, when the wind whispered through the trees, she thought she could hear Mamm's soothing voice and her baby sister's happy babble. But the fever had taken them both years ago. Catriona would never hear or see them again in this life.

She sighed.

The falconer family was not there. Perhaps they were late? Although she tried to suppress her imagination, it came to life as she turned back to arranging the baked goods in an attractive display. Suppose something had happened to Rabbie Graham? Catriona knew they went out hunting with the falcons. What if a hunter with a bow mistook the man for an animal and shot him? Her vision blurred with unshed tears at the thought.

Taking the edge of her apron, she dried her eyes, wiped her hands, and lined up the loaves of crusty bread side by side.

Da dumped rolls from a cloth sack into a large basket, giving her a nudge with his elbow. "The Graham family isna training today, but dinna fash yerself, they will return."

She shot him a look, afraid he was mocking her, but his bearded face was solemn and he gave her a wink.

"Da—" She stopped. What could she say? She couldn't tell her da, her best friend, that she yearned for Rabbie Graham or that she thought of him all day and dreamed of him at night. Before Rabbie Graham, Catriona had begun to dream of faceless men … a sign that she was now a woman, she supposed.

"Aye, Cat?" Thick black brows raised, Da's face reflected hope … hope that she would confide in him as she always did.

"Would ye pass me the scones, please?"

A twinge of guilt went through Catriona when her father's face fell with disappointment. But he leaned down, grabbed the bag of scones, and passed it to her.

Catriona took her time putting the scones in their basket one at a time. A woman with two young boys in tow came to the cart and drew Da's attention to serve them.

The castle's bakers provided bread for the nobles, and Catriona and her father sold their wares to peasants, servants, and others of lesser stations. Sometimes, the knights' wives would come to the bakery cart too.

Without the falconers for entertainment, the day seemed to last forever. Finally, the shadow grew long, and the last loaf of bread was sold. It was time to go home.

Catriona left out a faint sigh, careful to keep Da from hearing. Without Rabbie Graham to watch today, she felt as though a hole had been left in her heart. *Silly, Rabbie doesn't ken you even exist.*

After Catriona secured all the empty baskets on the cart, Da hitched up the donkey, and they headed toward the castle gate.

The road made a sharp turn and went downhill. Roger, the donkey, hated going through the two dark underground tunnels that were put there for security. The animal stopped, as usual, and Da had to coax him forward into the first damp, dimly lit passage. This happened again at the entrance to the second tunnel. Catriona didn't blame Roger. She pulled her wrap closer around her, happy to see the light and gatehouse at the end of the tunnel.

The two guards at the big stone gatehouse gave them cheery waves goodbye as Da led the donkey cart through the high, built-in archway. Right outside the main castle walls, they passed Benholm's Lodging, a five-story stone building that was cut into the rocky cliff. Catriona shivered, although it was not cold, and the sun still shone. There were bad men housed in Benholm's prison; men who had even done murder. She hoped to never set foot in that place, even though Da claimed the inn portion above ground was verra nice.

The road outside Dunnottar Castle dipped downward again under Catriona's feet in an even steeper decline. The castle was a big stone fortress sitting high on a rocky headland. It was surrounded by sharp cliffs that dropped into the North Sea. Traveling to and from the castle wasn't easy for anyone, but "outsiders" like Catriona and her father made their living from the coin spent by the castle dwellers.

Catriona hurried forward to take the donkey's reins from her father. He would need to walk beside the cart and apply the wooden brake handle if the vehicle picked up too much downhill speed. Roger would probably just keep walking all the way home without anyone to lead him, but they did it all the same. If something spooked the animal, he could take off running and destroy the old wooden cart. The clunky box with spoke wheels had belonged to Catriona's grandfather, and was the only way they could transport their baked goods to the castle.

When the path leveled off again, Da took her place at Roger's head, and Catriona was free to walk alongside the cart and daydream.

Perhaps Rabbie Graham would come and buy a loaf of bread tomorrow. Da said Rabbie's mother, Moira Graham, usually came for bread and rolls, but maybe she would send Rabbie instead.

She glanced down at her flour-soiled apron and plain green skirt. Putting a hand to her hair, she felt the many strands that had come loose from the braid. No, a castle-dweller, who was the son of the Grand Falconer, would never look twice at a common baker's daughter.

Och, you are just fooling yourself.

* * *

The daylong hunting trip for Sir Ogilvie and some of his noblemen had been a success. The falcons had brought down a dozen ducks and two cranes to grace the table of the governor and his guests.

Rabbie transferred the last of his lordship's hawks from the cadge, a rectangular framed perch that a servant wore hanging from two straps on his shoulders, and placed the bird in the specially designed traveling cage on the wagon.

"All set."

"Aye," Fin replied and clucked his tongue to drive the hitched team forward.

"I'll meet ye at home, Fin."

Fin acknowledged Rabbie's words with a wave as the wagon lurched off. Da had already left with the nobles in the hunting team, as befitting his status as Grand

Falconer. Sir Ogilvie's eagle rode on Da's horse. No common wagon would do for the lord's hunting bird.

Rabbie mounted his horse and whistled for Hamish. The dog had been sniffing around a bush and bolted over to him when summoned. With his falcon secured on the riding perch and his dog following, he set the horse in motion.

By now, he and his animals were alone. The setting sun glittered off the lake's surface, and Rabbie admired the beautiful scene for a second before turning toward home.

Sitting loosely in the saddle, Rabbie relished this time of solitude, surrounded by gradually thickening trees and the quiet peace of nature. Although he loved his family and appreciated the privileges of castle life, the noise and constant crowds were tiresome. Sometimes, he just needed to be alone to think.

Mamm had been hinting to him about settling down with a wife. As the eldest of the Graham children, he needed to be the first to marry. But suppose marriage was not for him? Finding a suitable lass wasn't easy. Plenty of pretty girls caught his eye, but none seemed exactly right.

He sighed.

His mother pressed him to woo the daughters of noblemen, but Da disapproved, saying, "Ye dinna want the lad to suffer the humiliation of rejection when he reaches above his rank."

Rabbie found himself smiling as he remembered the indignation his plump little mother displayed in defending him as a "comely lad" and a "good provider." But they both knew that Da was right; he had no title, no lands, and very little money to bring to a marriage. There was no reason for a titled man to give over his daughter to Rabbie Graham.

He shuddered.

Why was he even thinking of taking a wife? Mamm was getting into his head. There were more important things to consider, such as adding some new hunting birds —

The sounds of a woman's scream, something crashing through the underbrush, and Hamish's sudden barking shattered the peace.

Chapter 3

Rabbie quickly untied the jesses from the perch, removed Brisda's hood, took her on his ungloved wrist, and jerked his arm upward to release the falcon into the air. Ignoring the painful claw scratches on his exposed skin, he grabbed up the reins and urged the horse to a run.

Hamish, still barking, led Rabbie through the forest, over a small brook, and up a gentle incline as they followed the sound of the screams. He crested the top of the hill in time to see his spaniel lunge for the throat of a large, black boar with long, evil tusks. Not even ten feet away from the fighting animals, a big man lay on the ground with a woman beside him. Beyond them, a cart crashed through the woods, pulled by a donkey hell-bent on escaping.

The woman's frightened, pleading eyes met his for a split second before Rabbie pursed his lips and whistled Hamish away from the prey. *No time for hesitation.* He simultaneously drew his spear from its holder and threw it.

Hamish dropped his hold and backed off as the spear thunked into the boar's side. It let out a gurgling squeal and tried to run but dropped to the ground seconds later.

The donkey cart bounced away over the rocky ground. It would be torn to pieces if he didn't stop the headlong flight of the frightened animal.

Using his knees, he maneuvered the horse to the left and straight ahead, then sharply to the right to head off the donkey. They ran side-by-side until the cart finally slowed to a stop. One wobbly wheel came off the small cart and rolled off into the bushes just before the still-braying little animal drew to a stop.

The wheel could wait. Rabbie jumped off the horse, secured the donkey to a tree, leaped back on the horse, wheeled it around, and went back to where he had left the boar.

* * *

Catriona, sitting on the mossy ground and cradling her father's head, realized she had watched the man ride after their bakery cart with her mouth hanging open. She closed it.

As I live and breathe. 'Twas the falconer, Rabbie Graham ... I think.

The man had appeared then disappeared so quickly, she couldn't be sure.

"Da, Da, are ye all right?"

She stroked his bristly cheek with one hand. The dried leaves that cushioned his fall rustled and crackled as he stirred then abruptly sat up.

"What happened, Cat?"

"Roger got scairt when a big boar came out of the trees. See, over there—"

The sight just a short piece away gave them both pause. Sitting on top of the fallen boar, perched on its big belly, was a large peregrine falcon. A brown-and-white dog with floppy ears sat on the ground beside the two, its tongue lolling out and head tipped to one side. Both the bird and the dog regarded the two humans with bright, curious eyes.

"Where did those two come from, and who stuck that spear in yon beastie?" Da got to his feet slowly, leaning a bit on Catriona as she helped him up.

"Hamish and Brisda are mine and so is the spear."

Catriona swung around.

In the fading light, a horse and rider stepped out of the trees and approached. With each step closer, Catriona's heart beat faster.

The son of the Grand Falconer, Rabbie Graham, drew close and gazed down at them from astride his mount. She stopped breathing. Even in this dim light, his strikingly blue eyes stared into her soul. His brown hair, worn long in the style of the day, was tousled by his ride to their rescue.

Then he was off the sleek black horse and standing in front of them. "Are ye all right, sir?" He pointed off to their left. "Yon wagon will require a bit o' work. The wheel came off, but your steed is unhurt."

Da let out a hearty chuckle. "Imagine, Cat. He called that stubborn, fat-headed donkey a 'steed'." Her father held out a thick-fingered, hairy-knuckled hand. "I ken who you are. Thank ye, Master Robert Graham, yer help 'tis much appreciated. I'm Cináed Dunn and this is my daughter, Catriona."

Rabbie shook Da's hand enthusiastically and then turned to her and gave her a half bow. "Excuse me for asking, but ye both look verra familiar to me. Have we met before?"

"I ken ye havena been to the bakery cart for many years now, but ye used to come regular-like with yer mamm."

The smile on Rabbie's handsome face broadened even further. "I ken ye now, the baker and his lovely daughter."

Catriona drew in a deep breath, picked up her skirts, and dipped into a curtsy. The next thing she knew, Rabbie Graham had put a finger under her chin and gently pressed to draw her up again ... and he did it right in front of her father!

"I'm no man to be bowing to, Catriona Dunn." His voice was soft and gentle. "I am but a common working man."

Raising her head to meet his gaze, she had to blink to bring his face into focus.

He gave her a smile she would take with her to her grave. His expression was full of humility, kindness, and compassion with just a touch of rakishness. Then he dropped his hand and turned toward her father.

"If we work fast, Cináed Dunn, we may be able to fix that wheel before dark." With that, Rabbie passed over his horse's reins. She took them wordlessly.

Rubbing the back of his head, where Roger had hit him with his hard donkey skull and knocked him out, Da ambled off with Rabbie Graham to find the wheel. With a faint woof, the dog scrambled after them. Catriona was left with a horse, a falcon, and a dead boar that was already drawing flies ... every girl's dream.

Uncertain as to whether she should follow them or stay put, Catriona decided to remain behind. Still holding the horse's reins, she led it to a tree, tied it up, and sat down on a log. The falcon watched her for a few minutes before it began to peck at the boar's eyes. Catriona shuddered and turned away. She was not a squeamish woman, but some things made the bile rise in her stomach. Eyeballs fell into that category.

As the darkness deepened, Catriona's musing took a bad turn. *Suppose Da doesn't come back?* How would she find him? What would she do? She didn't know the way home. Why hadn't she paid attention instead of blindly following along, lost in daydreams?

Pulling her knees up to her chest, she huddled inside her cloak. *Will Rabbie Graham come back so I can see him again?* Oh my, his touch on her face had sent tingles all through her whole body. How could she get him to do it again? Och, what would Da say if he did?

Peering into the darkness, she could make out the hump that was the boar; she could no longer see the falcon. Perhaps it had left her too. Rabbie's horse snorted, so she knew it was still here. If they never came back, she would try to ride the beast home. The idea comforted her just a bit, but then again, she didn't know which way to go.

After what seemed like hours, the rumble of men's voices and creaking of wooden wheels reached her ears. Jumping to her feet, Catriona stomped the blood back into her legs and waited. A spot of light between the trees grew closer.

"Sorry we took so long, Cat. Yer ol' Da's back now."

Relief flooded through her and Catriona rushed forward to hug her big, solid father.

"I missed ye, Da."

His belly bounced up and down against her as he chuckled. "I'd never abandon ye, m'girl."

He released her and turned to the young man beside him. "We've much to thank ye for, Rabbie Graham. Without yer help, yon boar may have eaten my girl here."

By the light of the lantern hanging from a vertical pole on the cart, Catriona saw a big grin cross the handsome face of Rabbie Graham before he spoke.

"Och, 'tis nae a problem. Glad am I tae help."

On his gloved right hand, he held the beautiful gray peregrine falcon. It had found its master.

"I thank ye also, sir." Catriona gazed pointedly at the hunting bird. "If I may ask, what is the leather piece on your falcon's head?"

Rabbie stroked the bird's feathered breast with one finger. "That is called a hood, m'lady. It covers her eyes so Brisda will remain calm and ride peacefully on my hand or on her perch."

"Brisda is a verra pretty thing." Catriona wanted to touch the bird too, but dared not.

"Aye, that she is, but even pretty things can have sharp claws."

"Gloves like yers make sense, laddie," Da said.

"Aye." Rabbie walked over to his horse, transferred the falcon to its perch, took off the leather glove, and slid a large, glittering knife from his saddle.

"Would ye care fer some meat, Cináed Dunn?"

"I would."

Da gave the lantern to Catriona. She held it up and watched the two men quickly butcher the hog by the dim light. Rabbie took a smaller amount as would fit into his saddlebags, and they loaded the rest into the cart, leaving the carcass for the woodland creatures.

The awkward moment came for Catriona after the men had finished their work. She tried to act normally when Rabbie Graham approached, but her brain had turned to a jumble of thoughts, all dealing with the handsome man and his attractive, muscular form. She swallowed and attempted to loosen her tongue as she deliberately glanced beyond him to her father.

Even in the dim lantern light, her father's big toothy grin and nod spoke to her of his thoughts. He was encouraging her in this encounter.

Rabbie stepped in front of her and bowed at the waist then straightened. He was very tall, a whole head taller than she.

"'Twas a pleasure to meet ye, Catriona Dunn. I trust ye will welcome me at your bakery cart for a bit o' bread when next we meet?" She could swear he had a twinkle in his eye as he spoke.

Unable to control her mouth, Catriona grinned at him in return and dropped into a small curtsy. "A visit from ye would be most welcome, kind sir. Da and I thank ye again for your assistance tonight."

"That we do, lad. That we do." Cináed drew up beside Rabbie and clapped him heartily on the shoulder. Normally men would stumble at this unexpected masculine gesture, but Rabbie Graham didn't budge or even flinch under this assault. Catriona liked that. Her view of men had been shaped by her big, gentle father, and she discovered that she favored manly men. It seemed Rabbie might be one of them.

* * *

Despite his weariness, Rabbie locked his legs and stood his ground when Cináed Dunn wacked his shoulder. This particular gesture had been forced upon him in the past by his own father and brother. If Rabbie dared move an inch to keep his balance, Fin would be sure to jeer unmercifully.

With this thoroughly masculine test out of the way, Rabbie turned to Cináed with his right hand outstretched.

"Time to take my leave. Hamish and Brisda will appreciate the meat, as will I … cooked for me, of course."

The two men shook hands as Rabbie furtively watched the daughter in his peripheral view. *She seems very amiable and quite pretty. I believe getting to know this lassie would be very pleasant.*

"Are ye heading back to Dunnottar?" Cináed asked as he dropped Rabbie's hand and went to Catriona's side, pulling her against him protectively with an arm around her shoulders.

"Aye."

"Sleep well," the baker's daughter said.

As she spoke these words, an image of Catriona Dunn, naked in his bed with her black hair spread out on a pillow, popped into Rabbie's head. It was a very good thing Cináed was unable to read thoughts or Rabbie would be a dead man.

"Aye, and the same to ye. Have you far to travel yet? I've concern for yer welfare in Dunnottar Woods."

Catriona opened her mouth, but apparently changed her mind and closed it again.

He wondered what she had been about to say. Her father spoke up instead.

"I've traveled this path many a time. Catriona will be safe with me. We've only a few miles to go."

Rabbie nodded. "Well, guid evening to both of ye."

Tearing his eyes away from the lovely Catriona, whose dark hair and eyes shone in the lamplight, Rabbie then called to Hamish. The dog had wandered away in the darkness. Mounting his horse, he turned it toward Dunnottar and watched the baker and his daughter walk away with their donkey and meat-laden cart.

His dog came bounding through the fallen leaves with a small woof in greeting. Rabbie and his animals headed home. After the excitement of the past few hours, riding without human companionship seemed lonely. But a strange tingle of excitement niggled in his belly when he thought of buying a loaf from the bakery cart and seeing Catriona Dunn again.

Then he reflected on his own, very gregarious family, particularly his brother, Fin. This encounter was best kept to himself. The less they knew, the less they'd bother and tease him.

Chapter 4

The difficult climb up the steep stretch of road to Dunnottar Castle didn't seem nearly as hard this morning as it had the day before, even though Catriona had slept very little during the night. The encounter with the boar and the heroic actions of Rabbie Graham replayed in her head, making her toss and turn all night.

When Da woke her before daylight to help make the bread, her head seemed full of wool. A nice, strong cup of tea had helped, and now a new kind of excitement coursed through her veins. Never in her life had the very idea of seeing a man given her such trepidation. When she was younger, several boys had crossed her path because her mother loved to go and visit the neighbors. Often, Catriona would be forced to spend time with the sons of these women friends of her mamm. Not one had stirred her blood like Rabbie Graham, the falconer.

Early morning sun glittered off the surface of the North Sea, still visible on either side of the castle headland. A cool breeze blew off the water, and Catriona pulled her cloak closer around her with a shiver. Roger, the donkey, plodded along stoically, ignoring all around him as he towed the cart full of bread, pastries, and hard biscuits.

Da did almost the same thing, trudging along, lost in his own thoughts. Her big,

black-bearded father was very taciturn,
particularly in the morning.

"Guid morning, Dunn." The gatehouse
guard greeted them and waved them
through. The heavy iron portcullis had
already been raised to allow other merchants
to file into the castle grounds with their
wares.

"Guid morning to ye, sir," Da replied
with a tip of his hat as they passed by.

Catriona lifted the cloth covering the
basket of biscuits, pulled out two, and gave
one biscuit to each brawny, hairy guard. They
thanked her and immediately ate their gifts.

As the Dunns emerged from the last
tunnel into the sunshine, Catriona's pulse
quickened. Would the Graham family be out
here today working with their falcons?

"Calm yerself, Cat. Ye ken the falconers
donnae come out so early."

She jerked her head over to him as Da
winked at her with a little knowing smirk
under his black mustache.

"I'm not excited at all, 'tis just an
ordinary morning," she declared, tossing her
head.

"Aye, just any other day." He chuckled.

They positioned the cart in the usual
place, with the vegetable farmer on the right
and the herb woman on the left. Roger was
unharnessed, given his oats and a bucket of
water, and then left to nap the day away tied
to a post.

Catriona helped Da set up their baked
goods. At the front of the cart, in cloth-lined
baskets, rested the more costly wheaten bread

and manchet, which was their finest white bread. Behind those were the baskets of brown and black breads, common loaves, biscuits, scones, and a small supply of flaky apple pastries Catriona had made. The pastries were a new addition to their baked goods. If they sold well, she might make more. They were priced to sell to somewhat wealthier castle-dwellers, like the knights and noble families. Catriona secretly counted the Grand Falconers' family among this group, hoping to lure Rabbie Graham to their cart more than once with her tasty pastries. Da often told her to practice her cooking skills well because, "The way to a man's heart is through his stomach."

Until a few days ago, she hadn't cared much for the idea of winning any man's heart. Now, it seemed a desirable task.

She was, in a word, smitten.

After glancing toward the open area of the castle courtyard for the thousandth time, Catriona finally saw what she had been waiting for. The first ones to appear were Rabbie's red-haired sister and brother. They each carried a falcon, walked to the chest-high wooden cross bar mounted on a pole, and transferred the two birds to the perch.

Rabbie emerged from the doorway to the rectangular wooden building where the birds were kept, which people called the "mews."

"Cat. Cat."

Startled, Catriona turned to face her father. "What is it, Da?"

"We've a customer, *nighlean*." He pointed with his chin to the woman standing in front of Catriona who was holding two loaves of bread.

Heat crept up Catriona's neck and flooded her face. She had been caught staring at the falconers. *How embarrassing!*

"Aye, sorry, missus," she murmured. As she took the woman's coins, she silently vowed to make sure she focused on the reason she was here. Assisting her father run the business would be her only task, lest he find reason to leave her at home again.

She managed to keep her promise for almost two hours and served quite a few customers while glancing at the Graham family now and again.

"No, sir, there are no mealworms in our bread. If ye would like to pick out a loaf, I'll be glad to show you." Catriona had seen this particular man before. Dressed in tattered clothing, he appeared to be a poor peasant, but his manner of speaking belied that image. He had attempted to gain free bread from her Da using this very claim of mealworms only last week.

"Will ye give it to me at no cost, if I find worms?"

"No. 'Twill be fed to the hogs."

"But I need proof—"

A deep, familiar voice interrupted. "M'lady has told ye the truth. The Dunns sell the finest, freshest bread of Dunnottar's realm. Buy or be on yer way now."

Mumbling under his breath, the man paid his coins for the least-expensive common loaf and took his leave, tearing off chunks to eat as he walked away.

"Greetings, Catriona Dunn."

She smiled. "Guid morning to you, Rabbie Graham."

And he was a sight any warm-blooded woman would smile to see. The sun showed off reddish tints in his wavy brown hair that had been cut to fall just below his collar in the latest fashion. Twinkling blue eyes seemed to gaze straight into her soul. His handsome face showed a hint of the boy he had been and the man he had recently become.

Catriona had just remembered to breathe again when she realized how he was dressed. Rabbie Graham wore a snowy linen shirt under full Scottish regalia—blue-and-green tartan sash and kilt, white stockings with a *sgain dubh* knife in the top, sporran at the waist, and a gold broche on his sash.

She barely stifled a sigh of womanly appreciation. He had not been wearing this when first she saw him working his birds this morning.

"Have ye got something important to do today?"

Rabbie's dark eyebrows rose at her question. "No, why do you ask?"

She just let her eyes travel up and down the length of his person.

He grinned. "I was hoping ye'd notice me in this crowd." Rabbie waved one hand at the many people moving about the market area.

"Well, ye were successful. I did."

Then his gaze dropped to his shoes and up to her face again before he spoke quietly.

"Would your Da spare ye for a bit? Perhaps you'd like to see our falcons?"

* * *

As he waited for Catriona to talk to her father, Rabbie glanced across the bailey toward his family. His father had brought out Sir Ogilvie's golden eagle for a practice session. The majestic bird, with its dark brown feathers interspersed with light gold plumage, sat majestically on the main perch, still wearing a leather hood.

Rabbie wondered again if he had made the right choice in clothing today. His brother, Fin, had laughed; he did not understand Rabbie's need to appear before Catriona in fine fashion. A man had to find a way to impress a pretty lassie like Catriona before a knight of a higher station discovered her. Many young men either lived in or came to Dunnottar, and Rabbie was sure he would have to compete with every one of them. She was new to the castle and sure to be courted by the others.

He stiffened his spine and stood tall.

"Hello again, young Rabbie." Cináed Dunn held out a beefy hand so Rabbie gave it a firm shake. "I suppose Catriona can be spared for a bit. I will need her back to help with the mid-day selling."

Rabbie gave a solemn nod. "Aye, consider it done."

A big toothy smile creased the older man's face. "Off with ye both now."

Catriona glanced at Rabbie and smiled. His world seemed to flood with sunshine and his heart raced. How could one person's smile affect him so? Not surprisingly, his anatomy came to attention in that moment. Concealing kilts were a blessing to be sure.

They walked side by side toward the mews. Although Rabbie struggled mightily to form coherent thoughts, he could think of nothing to say. She smelled faintly of bread and flowers … a nice combination to his senses.

Ahead of them, Isobel was the only member of his family working outside at the moment. She sat on a wooden bench with her head down, absorbed with something on her lap, while the eagle patiently waited on its perch.

"Guid morning, Isobel," Rabbie called to get her attention.

She looked up. "Guid morning, Rabbie. Who have ye got with you?" His sister greeted Catriona with a smile, but her blue eyes showed how much her brother's actions had surprised her.

"Catriona, this is my sister, Isobel Graham. Isobel, this is Catriona Dunn, she is the baker's daughter. I thought she might like to see how we work and train the falcons for Sir Ogilvie and the nobles.

Isobel raised one auburn eyebrow and her gaze flicked over his formal Scottish regalia. "Aye, I was just fixing the lure. His lordship's eagle tore it off the line."

Rabbie held out a hand. "Let me see."

"'Tis already fixed." She placed the brown leather object, with a long string attached, into his hand. "Ye can practice the eagle. I will go help Fin with his work inside the mews." Isobel turned to Catriona. "Happy to meet ye, Catriona. I hope to see you later."

As he watched his sister walk away, he wondered what Catriona thought of the way Isobel dressed in breeches like a man. If his companion was outraged or surprised, she showed no sign.

"Please sit, m'lady." Rabbie injected a playful little bow as he waved her to the bench.

She gathered her skirts and sank onto the hard wooden surface, smoothing the dark green fabric over her knees.

Taking a deep breath and hoping the eagle would cooperate today; Rabbie proceeded to put the bird through her paces.

First, he donned a long, thick glove that covered his hand and up to his shoulder. Then he untied the jesses holding the bird to his perch and removed the leather hood allowing her to see again. Rabbie pointed out to Catriona how the eagle shook out her feathers in a gesture called *rousing*.

Keeping his gaze on the bird of prey, he walked backward about forty paces. Taking the long line with a lure on the end, he raised his arm and swung the lure in a large, slow circle over his head for a few revolutions. This was designed to capture the bird's attention.

Pursing his lips, Rabbie let out several short whistles, and then let the lure drop to the ground. The eagle cocked her head and lifted off the perch in a dramatic fashion.

He heard Catriona gasp as the bird spread her long wings and soared overhead.

Rabbie ran now, pulling the line and letting the lure drag along the uneven grass and dirt. Making a slow, wide arc, the eagle came back around and suddenly dropped to the ground, capturing the lure in its sharp talons.

As soon as the bird landed, Rabbie pulled a full-sized dead rat from his sporran. Clutching the food in his big glove, he called the eagle to his wrist using another series of short whistles. Once there, the eagle took the rat from him and ate it greedily.

* * *

Catriona couldn't take her eyes off this show. How amazing to get a wild creature to do your bidding!

Rabbie walked over and stopped in front of her, still holding the huge eagle effortlessly on his extended arm.

"Dinna touch her, but ye can come a bit closer to watch how she uses that powerful hooked beak to tear her prey into pieces she can eat."

Catriona slowly stood and moved one cautious step closer to watch the eagle eat the remains of the rat.

"Can you touch her?"

"Not while she's eating … no one can or should. Eagles are very strong and will protect their food."

They watched as the bird swallowed the last bit of the rat, fur and all.

"She ate the bones and fur!" Catriona looked to Rabbie for a response.

"Aye, birds cannae use that part, though. They will bring it back up later in the form of a pellet. Quite interesting to see how they can press it all together."

"'Tis verra interesting."

"Ye are a strange lassie, Catriona Dunn. Doesna the sight of the dead rat make ye queasy?"

She raised her head to meet his gaze with surprise. "Och, no. As a girl, I loved to wander in the forest and saw many dead things and creatures about. How do ye get this eagle to come back to your whistle?"

He smiled and her heart skipped a beat.

"All of our falcons are trained to chase and kill their prey, but they must relinquish it to us in exchange for easy food. They become accustomed to eating only what we give them. They are gluttons actually. Verra greedy things."

Rabbie reached into his sporran, drew out the leather hood, and slipped it over the sleek head of the eagle.

"Where do ye get the hoods?"

"We make them ourselves. Isobel made this one."

It was a small piece of leather with fine stitching, beautifully tooled design, and a jaunty little feather on top. The hood fit the bird's head perfectly.

"It is lovely, Rabbie." Catriona deliberately chose this moment to use the more familiar version of his name and watched him closely for any reaction.

The smallest twitch in the corners of his mouth told her that he did not mind.

"Would ye like to see where we keep the birds? We have quite a few."

"Aye." Catriona wasn't ready to leave his company. She glanced up at the sky. The sun had not reached its zenith yet. Da could do without her.

Chapter 5

"Da, did ye know that the Honours of Scotland are kept in Dunnottar? Just imagine, King Charles II used the very same crown, sword, and sceptre during his coronation, and now they are in a chest in the castle!"

Catriona sat across the table from her father. He industriously shoveled stew with boar meat into his mouth as he listened to her, nodding at intervals. She, on the other hand, could barely touch a bite of dinner in her excitement.

"Today, after we looked at the birds, Rabbie showed me around the palace—as much of the palace he was allowed to show me. He said he wasna permitted access to the whole building, just parts."

"Mmph."

"'Tis such a wonderful thing for Dunnottar Castle and for Sir Ogilvie to be entrusted with guarding sacred objects."

"Trouble waiting to happen, if ye ask me." Cináed mopped up gravy with a piece of common bread that had not sold.

Her fork stopped in mid-air. "Why, Da?"

He finished swallowing before regarding her solemnly. "With the English in Lothian, the Honours could not go to Edinburgh lest they be captured. The English have no love for our Scottish king. I wouldna be surprised if they wanted to destroy the regalia. Keeping them here means they are a secret. We all ken

39

how well secrets are kept. Wagging tongues will get Dunnottar into trouble yet."

"Och, nae, 'twill no be a problem, Da. Rabbie says the castle is well defended."

He waved a big hand dismissively. "That falconer is young and does not ken how relentless the English can be. If they want the Honours, nothing will stop them".

Catriona's exuberance began to fade in light of her father's skepticism. Now she felt foolish, like a silly girl, gushing over his golden words. She gazed down at the food in her bowl without seeing it. *Is this what attraction to a man does? It made me into a mindless person with no thoughts of my own. I will not allow it.*

"Och, lass, dinna fash yerself, young Graham may be right about the castle's defenses at that. Scots such as live in Dunnottar are fierce fighters."

Da's tone was gentle, the voice he often used to soothe her worries since Mamm had passed.

Allowing her body and face to relax, Catriona met his gaze and smiled. "'Tis right ye are too, Da. I've nae worries with you as my Da."

"That's me smart daughter. Your old Da would not let anything happen to ye."

Catriona nodded and began to eat her dinner again. Her father was a big, braw man, no doubt, but hadn't a well-placed stone knocked him senseless just days ago? He was as human as they all were.

* * *

Rabbie and the entire Graham family sat with Sir Ogilvie and the other nobles in the Great Hall to break their nightly fast. Eager plans were hatching for an upcoming hunt that would take place over the course of several days. They would be traveling a fair distance from Aberdeenshire and Dunnottar Castle.

An elbow poked Rabbie's side. "The Baron of Roslin is scairt of falcons," Fin whispered. "We should fly Brisda at his head and watch him scream like a bairn."

Rabbie didn't feel much like laughing at Fin's idea. Suddenly, it seemed childish to pull such pranks. Only last week, before he'd met Catriona Dunn, he and Fin had tried to embarrass a noble or two. The Baron of Roslin, by virtue of his height and width, was an especially good target. So far, they had managed to get Fin's peregrine to let loose with a big gob of waste right on the man's head, and Rabbie's dog, Hamish, could be commanded to stealthily steal Roslin's rare hunting catch before he could waddle over to retrieve it.

"Why do ye not fly your own falcon at his head? I've lost the taste for such tomfoolery."

Fin's twin red brows shot up. "We've had great fun with the wee man. Do ye have something against fun now?"

Rabbie shoved a piece of bread in his mouth and chewed as he eyed Fin. Every loaf or crumb of bread on the long breakfast tables reminded him of Catriona. He knew she hadn't baked these particular items, but she smelled of bread. He wondered if her mouth would taste like bread too. Catriona would not like to hear that he had fun over someone else's humiliation. Mother didn't like it. She had tanned their backsides many a time over the years for pulling pranks just like the ones Fin had suggested. Isobel never did such things, and she would never help the two of them with their nasty schemes.

Swallowing the lump of his newest favorite food, Rabbie turned to his brother.

"I just think it might be time to stop doing such childish things, Fin. I am three and twenty now, and a man. Men shouldna take advantage of the weak."

"Roslin isnae weak, just gullible and slow."

"Ye ken what I mean, Fin."

Isobel's face appeared as she leaned over to regard Rabbie with Fin between them. Her bright blue eyes sparkled merrily. "He means he's sweet on Catriona Dunn and wants to impress her."

A grin stretched across Fin's pale face, so similar to their sister's with bright blue eyes and freckles included. They both clearly favored their father, Boyd, in coloring.

Rabbie had their mother, Moira's dark hair, with Da's blue eyes.

As if Rabbie's thoughts had summoned the man, Boyd Graham, Grand Falconer of the realm, stood in front of them, hands planted on the table, leaning toward his children.

"I want Isobel and Fin to help your mamm prepare and pack what we'll need for this three-day hunt coming up."

"What about Rabbie, Da?" Fin already had a rebellious gleam in his eye over this news. "Rabbie will be going out to find eyasses. We need to get the young ones before they begin to fly …"

"… but when they're old enough to ken that they are falcons." Isobel finished Da's sentence for him, then sighed. "Why can't I go, Da? I like the fuzzy chicks, and I can climb as well as Rabbie."

"You'll be getting your chance, Isobel, but not this time." Da eyed them each in turn with a no-nonsense stare from under his red, bushy brows. "Do I make myself clear, falconers?"

"Aye, Da." Rabbie answered for all of them, as was his normal practice.

Boyd nodded and turned to leave with a swish of his kilt, but Rabbie spoke up again quickly. "Uh, Da, might I bring a friend to help me hunt eyasses?"

"Seems a braw idea. Better to hunt in pairs. Why didn't I think of it?" The corners of Boyd Graham's mouth lifted to reveal straight white teeth and his eyes crinkled in the corners. Then his brows drew together. "This friend wouldn't be Fin, would it? Moira will tan my hide if she does not get his help."

"No, 'tis someone else."

"I ken who—" Rabbie clapped a hand over Isobel's mouth. She glared daggers at him, but Da had already turned away when one of the nobles called him over.

"Hush, both of ye." Rabbie stood and moved directly behind his siblings, bent and pulled their heads close to his. "I'll make it up to ye and take your turns cleaning the mews. Just one turn each, mind."

This seemed to placate them and both agreed to keep quiet on the identity of the "friend."

"Here comes Mamm. Time to go," Fin warned.

The three younger Grahams scattered in different directions.

Rabbie looked back to see their plump little mother standing in the middle of the Great Hall with her hands on her hips and staring at them. He kept moving.

* * *

"Keep watch and give a shout, if you see the mother falcon coming."

Catriona tipped her head back to see the nest Rabbie had pointed out high in the cliffside. "I'll try my best, but you know how fast these birds fly."

"Aye, I'm quick with my hands and can drop an eyass into the cage verra fast."

She looked at his hands then. Odd how she hadn't noticed before how long his fingers were, not stubby and fat like her Da's. He held a small wooden cage, which he proceeded to drop into a cloth bag that closed with a drawstring. Slinging the bag over one shoulder, Rabbie then gave Catriona a smile.

"I am ready. Will ye watch out for me?"

"Oh, yes."

She watched all right. Nothing could have taken her attention away from the man as he climbed the cliff. Each time he reached for the next handhold, she held her breath until he had safely attained the new height.

Catriona pulled her cloak closer against the wind and scanned the blue sky in all directions. No adult falcon appeared yet. A few smaller birds dipped and climbed in the cool air.

"Are ye all right, Rabbie?"

"Aye, I've found three nestlings." His voice could barely be heard as the breeze carried it away. "We'll leave two here."

As she kept a close watch on him, hanging onto the side of a cliff like the scrubby bushes that grew out of the cracks in the stone, she wondered what she would do if he fell. Was this something his whole family did to get new birds, or was it just Rabbie who risked his life?

Catriona could barely stand this anxiety, but she didn't regret coming with him for a second.

Riding here behind him on the horse, with both arms around his waist and her head resting against his back, had been the most wonderful thing she had ever experienced in a physical manner. The warm, solid strength of the man wrapped in her arms almost took her breath away. The way he occasionally put a hand over hers and gently squeezed, told her he was happy she had come.

Da had been unhappy about allowing this unchaperoned adventure, but had finally relented after she pleaded and promised to be virtuous and proper.

Catriona wanted to hide her face with embarrassment when Da not only lectured Rabbie about behaving properly, but also insisted on speaking to Moira Graham. Thankfully, Rabbie's mother had given her solemn word that she knew her son to be honorable and true, and no harm would come to his daughter.

A noise sounding suspiciously like a gasp came from high above. She shaded her eyes and peered up the cliff.

"Watch out below!"

A split second later, the wooden cage crashed to the ground and splintered into pieces.

"Rabbie! Rabbie! Are you all right?" She ran closer to the sticks, but could see no signs of a baby falcon. Why had he dropped the cage?

High up on the craggy cliffside, the dark figure of a man moved nimbly from one foothold to the next, lower and lower. Rabbie dropped to the ground a few minutes later, and landed on his feet.

"Come on, Cat." He rushed over and took her by the arm. "We've got to get back to Dunnottar right now." His voice was full of urgency and his blue eyes were wide.

"Why? What is the matter?" She stumbled over the uneven ground as he practically dragged her over to the horse and threw her up on it before mounting behind her.

"We've got to warn them. English soldiers are camped just beyond that hill...thousands of them."

Chapter 6

The ground and the horse's hooves blurred before her tearing eyes as they flew along. Catriona held onto the pommel with both hands. She was grateful for the strong arm keeping her on the animal. Rabbie's thigh muscles flexed against her hips as he directed the horse, holding the reins in his right hand with his left hand against her ribs.

Catriona held her breath and hung on as the animal gathered itself then leaped over a log. She screamed as the return to earth nearly bounced her off were it not for Rabbie's strength. Maybe it would not be so bad to face the English compared to falling off and being trampled to death!

But she had a suspicion that Rabbie wouldn't leave her behind, and he needed to warn Dunnottar Castle. So she tried to tighten her leg muscles around the sweating horse.

Minutes later, they were forced to slow as the creature labored up the steep incline to the entrance. A faint and unpleasant odor rose from the poor animal, not totally unlike the odor of the perspiring man behind her.

"Come on, come on," Rabbie muttered, urging on the horse as he spoke his first words since they had rushed away.

From living with a taciturn father for years, Catriona knew that now was not the time for questions, though she was fairly bursting with them.

What were the soldiers doing? Why did they come? Would they hurt the Dunnottar Scots?

The horse could no longer be urged to run. The slanted road to the Dunnottar gatehouse had done its job.

"Ho ye! Ho ye, Shamas! Ho ye, Ian!" Rabbie yelled to the two gatehouse guards. At his urgent shout, they rushed into the road with broadswords at the ready.

Rabbie slid off the horse and gathered the reins.

"Shamas! Ian! The English army is camped about seven miles away down in the valley, near the ridge."

Uncertainty rooted Catriona to the spot and tied her tongue. But she didn't have to worry; Rabbie and the two guards knew what to do. Ian took off running into the castle.

"Show me where, lad." Shamas came closer and met Catriona's gaze where she still sat on the horse, but he said nothing to her.

"I'll need a fresh horse."

"Aye, that ye will. We'll have one ready at the stables. Meet me here with the other men." Shamas turned and gave hurried instructions to a young boy, who ran off inside the castle too.

"I'll be seeing Catriona to her Da before I go," Rabbie said to Shamas.

"No, dinna worry about me, Rabbie. I can find my father easy enough."

He made no answer. Taking the reins, he led the weary horse through the big stone gateway.

Catriona felt a bit foolish sitting atop his horse and riding while Rabbie walked, but she had no desire to go against his wishes, and he had not told her to dismount.

They reached the first tunnel and descended into its damp, gloomy depths, moving at a fairly good rate. Suddenly he stopped and came around to the side of the horse. She bent her head to look down at him. Lines between his dark brows spoke of the anxious situation that he seemed to comprehend better than she did.

"Oh, Rabbie!" She put out a hand to touch his face. "'Twill be all right. Aye?"

Before she realized what was happening, he had reached up, plucked her from the saddle, and allowed her body to slide down the front of his until her feet touched the ground. Her heart pounded at the sensation of his hard body against her breasts and belly.

He put a finger under her chin and tipped her head up to meet his earnest blue eyes. "May I kiss ye, Catriona? I've wanted to since we first met. It may be some time before I get the chance again."

"Och, yes. I've been dying to kiss ye too. Do ye think the English will —"

Her words were swallowed up as his mouth came down to settle gently on hers. The warmth of his lips sent a rush of heat swirling around in her abdomen. His tongue teased and probed at the entrance, so she let him in. The heady experience of the sweet sensations he evoked in the sensitive regions of her mouth had her reeling. Tendrils of hair fell around her face as his fingers loosened the braid she had wound around her head.

Could a person melt? Catriona vaguely wondered as she leaned into his body. Only his arm wrapped around her held her in a standing position.

His mouth left hers and disappointment took hold. But as she heard the sounds of men talking and horse bridles jingling, she realized why he had broken their embrace.

In the dim torchlight of the dark tunnel, two riders and a riderless horse approached.

"Rabbie Graham? Shamas sent us to find ye. He said ye'd seen English soldiers?" A tall, broad figure loomed over them in the semidarkness.

As he stood beside her, Catriona noticed the subtle stiffening of Rabbie's bearing as he drew himself up to his full, very tall height.

"Aye, I did, and I can show ye where they are."

"Well, get on with it now," the lead horseman said.

The men wore armor breastplates with their kilts and carried a multitude of weapons—broadswords, quivers of arrows and bows, axes, and other nasty-looking things she couldn't name.

Rabbie had nothing, no protection or weapon save the *sgian dubhh* she knew he had tucked in the top of his knee-high stocking.

"Catriona, will ye please take the horse to my Da and tell him where I've gone?"

She nodded, her throat tightening now with the sudden urge to cry.

He gave her a quick smile and ran to mount the spare horse. "I'm sorry I canna escort ye back to yer Da. I'll stop by and give him my apologies on my return."

"Be safe, Rabbie Graham." She managed to force the words out of her throat then raised a hand in farewell.

The Dunnottar men started forward, heading out of the castle. Rabbie hung back for just a bit, long enough to wave back at her and blow her a quick kiss before hurrying his horse to catch up with the men-at-arms.

By the time Catriona, blinking in the daylight, led the horse out of the second tunnel, she had gotten her emotions under outward control. Fear and anxiety twisted her insides.

Chaos reigned inside Dunnottar's courtyard. A woman carrying a small child ran past Catriona. She was screaming, "The Redcoats will kill us all. The Redcoats will kill us all." She yelled it repeatedly as she ran. Dogs and chickens seemed to be running in all directions with no particular destination. People, both old and young, did the same. A wagon full of barrels rumbled past, barrels dropped off the back as it careened toward the tunnels.

Obviously, news of the English soldiers had spread.

Pulling the prancing, rearing horse through the mob, Catriona struggled to keep hold of its reins. The whites of its eyes showed all around as it shied away from every new threat.

A big, hairy arm reached past her and grabbed the reins.

"Cat! Give it to me!"

Da had come to her rescue. She let go gratefully. Her arm strength had about reached the limit.

"I'm taking it back to the falconers, Da. It's Rabbie's horse." She had to yell to be heard above the noise.

With a strong yank, Da jerked the horse's head down and then threw one of their bakery cloths over its head. It stopped still, frozen in its blindness.

After murmuring a few words of reassurance to the animal, they were able to proceed.

"Where is the lad? How could he leave you to fight through all this?" He waved a hand at the riotous crowd. "Word of the English soldiers has everyone in an uproar. We're to stay inside the castle walls tonight."

Moving closer to her father, she grabbed his free arm and hung on tightly against the tide of frightened humanity. "Rabbie is the one who found the English soldiers, Da. He climbed up the cliffside to get a baby falcon and saw the campsite down in the valley. He's gone out with the Dunnottar guards to show them the location."

She glanced up at her father's familiar face and was thankful for his presence. "Rabbie says there are more English than we have warriors and nonwarriors combined … I'm scairt."

"Nae worries, daughter, yer Da is here."

But Catriona knew that even her big, strong father couldn't take on a whole army.

After tying the horse to a post near the falcon mews and taking the cloth off its head, they walked to the nicely carved front door of the Graham home.

Da knocked on the door.

Moira Graham opened the door and smiled brightly at seeing Catriona and Da there. Then she looked past the Dunns and her plump face fell. "That's Rabbie's horse. Where is he?"

"Moira, Catriona says that Rabbie, as the man who spotted the English soldiers, is showing the Dunnottar men-at-arms where the camp is located."

The older woman's hand slapped against her heart. "My son!"

Rabbie's sister appeared beside her mother. "What is the matter, Mamm?"

After Da repeated the news again, Isobel quickly drew her mother back and opened the door wider. "Please come in, my Da needs to hear this too."

The Graham home exuded cozy comfort. A fire blazed on the huge stone hearth and thick, braided rugs covered the floors. Whether it was the room or the people living here, Catriona felt welcome and peaceful here, as if she were in her own little cottage.

Boyd and Fin Graham, who had both been sitting in the stuffed chairs by the fire, came over to join the group near the door.

So, Cináed repeated the story to Rabbie's father and brother, and Catriona added a few facts here and there.

"Och, Rabbie will be fine. He's out there with Ogilvie's men-at-arms, Moira, dinna fash yerself. Remember, he is a man now. Many thanks fer returning his horse, Dunns. Fin will see it is stabled." Boyd glanced at his son, who spun heel and left through the front door.

"Well, that's that. We've said our peace and will be taking our leave now. Thank ye, Moira, for admitting us into yer lovely home." Da, not being a man with numerous social skills or a desire to hold long talks, effectively put an end to this conversation. Catriona didn't let her disappointment show. She had hoped to stay longer and spend more time with Rabbie's family.

"Yes, thank ye, Missus Graham." She smiled at them all. "Guid evening."

She and Da turned toward the door.

"Wait!"

They both froze at Moira Graham's command and turned back to the family gathered in the small entranceway.

"Sir Ogilvie has ordered everyone to stay inside Dunnottar's walls, isn't that right?" Moira said.

"Aye, 'tis so," Da agreed.

"Where will ye sleep tonight? If ye've nae place in mind, we've room for ye both here."

"You'd be welcome to stay." Boyd Graham nodded, glancing at his wife with approval in his blue eyes.

"Catriona can stay in my room." Isobel's face shone with a girlish excitement at the prospect.

Catriona hoped her Da would agree. Although the Graham house was not as grand as the palace Rabbie had showed her, with its tapestries on the walls and well-polished furniture, it was far nicer than the baker's cottage. She had no desire to huddle in the bakery cart all night with the Dunnottar gates closed for the night.

"I've got to retrieve Roger, he's still in the marketplace." Da's bushy black brows drew together with concern.

"Is that your son, Dunn?"

"No, sir, that would be my donkey."

Boyd Graham laughed and draped an arm around Da's big shoulders, drawing him deeper into the room. "It's settled then. Both of ye will spend the night here. When Fin gets back, I'll send him to fetch your donkey and stable him with the horses." Rabbie's Da clapped Catriona's Da on the back. "Now then, Cináed, how about a wee drop o' whiskey?"

Da chuckled and allowed himself to be led toward the big fireplace, shedding his coat as he went. "Sounds a braw idea to me."

"Come with me." Isobel grabbed Catriona's hand and led her down a short hall.

Will this night be enjoyable with the Graham family, or will it last far too long? And when will Rabbie come back? Catriona sighed inwardly and turned her attention to the very chatty Isobel.

Chapter 7

Night still cloaked the castle when Catriona awoke with no idea where she was. A few befuddled moments later, she realized that Isobel Graham, Rabbie's sister was the slightly snoring lump beside her. With a shiver, Catriona found out why she had awakened. Isobel had taken all of the blankets, and why not? The girl, at nineteen, was only two years younger than Catriona, and she was certainly accustomed to having the blankets and bed all to herself.

By the faint light of the moon shining outside the window, Catriona located another blanket she had seen draped over a chair back and used it to cover up. The Grand Falconer's daughter had luxuries Catriona did not possess. This sinfully soft feather-stuffed mattress was far superior to her crackly hay-stuffed mattress. The borrowed nightgown, with its soft material and fine stitching caressed her body like a lover ... or so Catriona imagined. She had no experience to know for sure.

Snuggling down under the covers, she mentally chastised herself for the wicked envy filling her. *I am a baker's daughter, no more, no less. I should be thankful that the Grahams allowed us to stay. I should not be covetous of their things.* Truly, only a small twinge of jealousy dwelled inside her. What she really coveted was Isobel's brother. She wanted Rabbie Graham.

No sooner had Catriona drifted off to sleep when a loud commotion somewhere in the house woke her. Men's voices, raised and urgent, woke Isobel as well. She jumped out of bed and grabbed her nightrail then pulled it on hurriedly.

"Come, Cat, we need to see what is happening."

Catriona wrapped the blanket around her like a shawl and followed the barefoot redhead.

By the flickering light from the fireplace, a small group of men could be seen gathered by the door. Rabbie's mother stood slightly outside this group, her face pale and anxious.

Isobel hurried to her mother's side. "What is it, Mamm?"

"Och, Belle, 'tis Rabbie; he's been captured by the English soldiers. They're sending more men to get him back, and they want Rabbie's falcon to help find him."

Isobel put her arms around her shorter mother and gathered her close.

Catriona could do nothing but stare. All coherent thoughts had fled, and it seemed her strength had left her body as well. She locked her legs and grabbed a nearby wooden pillar for support. *Rabbie captured? What would the English want with a falconer? How could this have happened?*

Da came up beside her. "Buck up, lass. Ye must appear strong for the Graham family." His whispered request sent shivers down her spine, and she stood tall again.

Rabbie's father spoke to the two kilted, sword-bearing men-at-arms. Fin, looking

DIANE WYLIE

rather grim also, stood with the men. The rest of them waited, stunned into silence. They watched Boyd Graham open the door and bid the men farewell.

Boyd closed the door and turned to his family and houseguests. "The Dunnottar warriors were shown the location of the English by our Rabbie. They instructed him to wait behind while they snuck down to the camp for a closer look. When they came back, Rabbie was gone and the earth was torn as in a fight. The two Dunnottar men searched for an hour and watched the camp, but couldna find the lad."

He paused for a second, seemingly to gather his strength and drew a deep breath. "They're hoping his falcon will lead us to him. We'll set Brisda loose at first light and pray she finds her master."

*　*　*

The first evidence that Rabbie had not died came in the form of someone singing a drinking song.

*Be merry, my hearts, and call for your quarts,
And let no liquor be lacking. We have gold in store; we purpose to roar,
Until we set care a-packing. There, Hostess, make haste, and let no time waste,
Let every man have his due. To save shoes and trouble, bring in the pots double.
For he that made one made two.
I'll drink up my drink, and speak what I think,
Strong drink will make us speak truly. We cannot be termed all drunkards confirmed,*

So long as we are not unruly. We'll drink and be civil, intending no evil.

If none be offended at me, As I did before, so I'll add one more

And he that made two made three.

The greedy curmudgeon sits all the day snudging at home with brown bread and small bear,

To coffer up wealth, he starved himself, scarce eats a good meal in a year.

The second hint was the horrific headache pounding his skull and a very sore spot on the back of his head.

But before he moved a muscle and let his captors know he was awake, he cracked open his eyes just a bit to look around. In a minute or so, his sight adjusted to the darkness.

He lay on his side on the ground, a clump of grass served as a resting place for his rope-bound wrists. Someone had taken his boots and nice warm coat, leaving him barefoot and shivering in shirtsleeves and breeches. Wind rustled through nearby trees and made tents flap. In his line of sight were a multitude of tents, campfires, and red-coated men.

The lousy cowards had bashed him on the head from behind, never giving him a chance to fight back. Where were the Dunnottar men? Perhaps they'd made it back to warn the castle.

Inch by inch, he raised his knees and strained to reach the rope around his ankles with his fingers.

"If you bloody well think you are going to escape, think again."

The English-accented voice came from behind Rabbie, followed by a sword tip that thunked into the ground in front of his nose. Reflexively, he jerked his head back and tried to roll away, only to be jerked to a stop by the rope that went from his wrists to a nearby tree.

The man laughed a deep and harsh sound with no humor in it. "Tied like a dog. Woof. Woof, Scottish scum."

Humiliation burned on top of Rabbie's anger. "What do ye want from me?"

The rope attached to his wrists began to move. In the dim moonlight, Rabbie watched it shorten. Jerking his head around, he saw the man, a beefy red-coated soldier, hauling on the trope looped over a thick branch high in the tree. Realizing what was going to happen, Rabbie braced his feet and tried with all his might to resist, to no avail. Slowly, painfully, he was hauled across the uneven ground and strung up off his feet by his wrists.

* * *

Catriona put on her shoes and stood. As she walked, she smoothed her skirt. Just a she put a hand on the doorknob, hushed voices outside caught her attention.

"Our Rabbie cannae have serious intentions toward this baker's daughter."

Catriona pressed her ear to the door. The voice sounded like Rabbie's mamm.

"I dinna ken, Mamm. She's verra nice and pretty too."

"Well, I'll no be having my firstborn marrying below him. The Baron of Roslin has a daughter. I've a mind to make a match there."

Rabbie's sister made a derisive sound before responding. "Likely his daughter is just as obnoxious as he and likely the Baron willna want a falconer like our Rabbie to wed his precious daughter. Rabbie will …"

Her voice faded away as the two moved farther from the door.

Moira Graham had been so kind. Catriona thought that Rabbie's mamm liked her. Hurt tightened her chest and she had to blink away a rush of tears. Then she straightened her spine and took a deep breath. *Rabbie will decide who he likes, and I think he likes me.* She stepped out of the room wearing a smile.

Only an hour had passed since the Dunnottar guards had left the Graham home. The women had packed food while the men prepared the falcons and horses for the trip.

Now Catriona, Moira, and Isobel stood outside. They were dressed and bundled in their long dark cloaks to watch the men getting ready to leave. Rabbie's dog, Hamish, danced around the group, excited and ready to be off.

"But, Da, I am as capable as Finn with the falcons. Can ye let me come? I'm already dressed for travel." Isobel opened the front of her cloak to reveal her customary boy's breeches, shirt, and boots.

"No, Isobel, I willna allow it. Ye must stay here to protect yer mamm." Her father's firm tone carried to where Catriona stood.

Moira put her hands on her hips and huffed. "Dinna fash yerself, Boyd Graham. I can take care—"

"Attack! They're attacking!" Someone yelled.

Boom!

Dirt and rocks exploded in the courtyard not far from where they stood. One of the horses shrieked and reared as Fin hung onto its reins and battled for control.

Zing! Zing! Zing!

Arrows flew over the wall arching down into the courtyard.

Catriona watched in horror as an arrow came down and impaled itself into Cináed Dunn's chest. She ran to his side as he crumpled.

"Da! Da!"

"Everyone inside! Let the falcons loose, Fin!" his father commanded.

Boyd, Moira, and Catriona grabbed Cináed's arms and pulled him toward the door. Isobel ran to help her brother.

Thunk!

With a gasp, Rabbie's mother fell on top of Da with an arrow protruding from her back.

"Moira!" Boyd ran to his wife.

Catriona was left alone to move her father to safety. She couldn't budge him. Tears streamed down her face as she fell to her knees and took him in her arms.

"Oh, Da, please don't leave me!"

His eyes met hers. To her horror, she could see the light fading already from those dark irises and his face was white. He struggled to speak even as blood trickled out of his mouth. "Goodbye, my Cat. I-I love ye, *nighean*. Stay …"

The light went out and he said nothing more.

With a moan, Catriona threw herself on top of her father and sobbed.

"Come with me!" Catriona didn't even look up at Isobel's shouted command. Arrows continued to fall around them and chaos had erupted in the castle courtyard. People and animals screamed, cannon fire thundered from outside the castle walls, and the smell of burning things choked the air.

A hand jerked her up by the arm and pushed her forward. She stumbled over the hem of her dress and nearly fell. Isobel grabbed Catriona's braid and pulled so hard that she had to follow or end up scalped.

Back inside the Graham house, the sounds and smells outside were slightly muted, and Catriona continued to sob. As soon as Isobel released her hold, Catriona collapsed into an emotional puddle on the floor.

"Oh, Da," she sobbed.

"Mamm. Oh, Mamm, please don't die."

"Hold on, Moira, we'll get help."

Catriona recognized Isobel and Boyd speaking, but the third sound was the cry of a wounded man—Fin.

Allowing herself just a few more sobs for now, Catriona struggled to get control.

Maybe she should help Rabbie's mother and family. Brushing the wetness from her face, she lurched to her feet. The three uninjured Graham family members huddled around the form of Moira Graham, who was lying on the floor with the arrow still protruding from her back. As soon as she saw the woman, Catriona knew Moira had passed from this earth. The shocked expression had frozen on her face, and the open eyes held no spark of life.

Catriona glanced at Boyd, who shook his head. His blue eyes, so much like Rabbie's, were red-rimmed and filled with tears.

"First Rabbie and now Cináed and Moira. They will pay." Boyd's words came out low and menacing.

"I'm going after them now!" Fin attempted to brush past his father, but was brought up short by a grab to his arm.

"Ye'll not be charging out there, reckless. I'll not lose another member of my family."

Isobel kneeled beside Moira's body, rocking and sobbing for her mother.

Tear streaked Fin's face and he glanced down at his mother's body. "What is yer plan, Da?" he croaked hoarsely.

How could they find Rabbie now with his falcon gone and the English at the gates? Catriona backed up until she hit the wall. How could she go home now? What about Da? Her throat closed convulsively. Her beloved father was gone in the blink of an eye. She was now orphaned. Alone. She slid down to the floor, hugged her knees, and sobbed for her lost Da.

Outside the house, shouting and booming sounds continued. Horses and wagons clattered past.

The front door flew open with a bang.

Everyone turned to stare at the newcomers. A woman, dressed in a green velvet gown with sleeves hanging to the floor, entered first. A fur-lined sumptuous cloak covered her gown. It was the lady of the castle, Lady Elizabeth Douglas Ogilvie, Sir George's wife. Two knights in full armor followed behind her, bearing an ornate wood trunk.

Catriona recognized that trunk right away. Rabbie had shown it to her only a few days before. It contained the Honours of Scotland.

Chapter 8

Catriona scrambled to her feet and curtsied as the woman passed by. Lady Ogilvie glanced from Moira's body to the falconers and back again.

"I'm so sorry for your loss, Grand Falconer."

The lady pushed back the hood of her cloak to reveal perfectly coiffed, shining brown hair bedecked with green ribbons woven through the intricate style.

Then she put a hand out, and Rabbie's father took it to help her as she knelt beside his wife and said a quick prayer. All heads bowed.

"Thank you, m'lady," Boyd said as he helped her to stand.

"Many more will be lost in this battle, I fear. The siege has stopped for now, so I used this chance to visit you. I have a favor to ask."

"Anything," Boyd's voice was stronger now.

"I have heard that your brave son is missing after leading our men to the English camp."

"To my sorrow, ye've heard correctly."

As his father spoke, Fin brought over a chair, and their guest gathered her skirts to sit. Lady Ogilvie looked back at the knights, caught sight of Catriona standing by the wall, and smiled slightly. Then she waved the two knights over. They placed the trunk at her feet.

Catriona moved a bit closer for a better view.

One of the knights opened the trunk lid.

Daylight streaming in through the windows illuminated the scene and caught the gleaming objects within the chest. Nestled on velvet pillows were the crown, sceptre, swords, and scabbard—the Scottish Regalia, also called the Honours.

Why Lady Ogilvie had brought the Honours here, Catriona had no idea nor did she care. While everyone was distracted, she moved slowly along the wall then slipped out of the door.

Outside, she found that the castle inhabitants had become more organized and orderly. Groups of people had already begun to clean up the rubble. Two men had loaded Da's body onto a litter. She ran to them.

"That's my father. Where are ye taking him?" Her voice cracked so she cleared her throat.

"Och, so sorry for yer loss, lassie. Come with us to the kirk. The dead will be blessed there and prepared for burial.

In a state of strange detachment, Catriona followed. They led her to a small stone church within the walls of Dunnottar. Catriona sat where she was told to sit, provided her father's name and particulars when asked by the priest, and watched him write this in his book. She wondered if her soul had somehow left her body to join her Da's soul … except her body was still alive.

People came and went. They spoke to her in gentle soothing tones, but their words made little sense to her. An older woman in a dark blue kirtle motioned to her now as Catriona sat alone in the kirk pew staring mindlessly at a shattered stained-glass window.

Obediently, she trailed the woman to a small room. Two large candles stood against the wall, framing the large colored windows showing angelic cherubs with trumpets to their lips. Candlelight cast the room in a warm glow that belied the cold temperature of the place.

The woman pulled back the cloth shroud covering a large lumpy form on a table.

"Is this Cináed Dunn, the baker and your father?"

His face had frozen into the same sad expression she had seen as life left him.

She swallowed and nodded.

"Come with me, child." The woman covered Da's face again and motioned to the two men in the shadows that Catriona had not noticed until they moved.

They picked up the litter and carried the shrouded body out of the room. Catriona followed, walking beside the woman.

An odd aura of calm and peace seemed to emanate from this woman of God. Catriona knew she should ask for the woman's name, but her mind refused to command the action.

Numbly, she put one foot in front of the other until they all entered the kirk's graveyard. She hadn't taken her eyes off her father's form. This would be the last time she ever saw her beloved Da.

A shiver ran through her, and then her cloak settled around her shoulders. Catriona glanced back in surprise. Fin had brought it here for her and covered her with it. He gave her a weak smile and walked over to join what was left of his family.

The Grahams were gathered beside two yawning rectangles in the ground. Catriona's mind clicked into some semblance of focus. They were here to bury their mother and wife, just as she was here to witness the burial of her father.

Rabbie's father, his sharp features softened by grief, came to her, put an arm around her shoulders, and drew her to a spot between the two open graves. Isobel and Fin joined them and took up positions on Boyd's other side.

Together, they watched and prayed as Cináed Dunn and Moira Graham were laid to rest in Dunnottar Castle's tiny cemetery.

* * *

Something cold and wet fell on the back of Rabbie's neck and on his bare shoulders. Then a hand slapped him hard across the face, jerking his head to the side. Some of the fog in his brain lifted at the pain. Tiny snowflakes dropped down gently, melting quickly on his skin.

"You'd be smart to tell me what I bloody well need to know, Scottish bastard. Our troops will be getting into Dunnottar soon, whether you talk or not. It will be far better to tell me where those crown jewels are hidden now or men will die if we have to search for them." The man, who had hung him up by his wrists and stripped off his shirt, sneered into his face. Droplets of spittle flew from the man's flapping lips.

Didn't this man know that Scots were a stubborn lot?

Rabbie shook his aching head. "Ye'll not get that information from me."

Without another word, the English soldier cracked a horsewhip across his back.

"Speak!"

Rabbie bit his lip.

Crack!

"Speak!"

The whip fell again and again. As his body jerked involuntarily in response to the painful assault, Rabbie redirected his mind to think of soft, lovely Catriona. Maybe the possibility of spending time with her would be more than a fleeting dream, if he survived.

* * *

"Please let her come, Da. Catriona's all alone and our Rabbie loves her. He told me so. We cannae leave her here alone to be captured if the English overrun the castle. Do it for Rabbie."

Isobel probably didn't realize or maybe she didn't care that Catriona could hear every word the lass said to her father. Those two were in the next room talking while Catriona and Fin stuffed food into sacks.

Catriona wrapped some salted boar meal in oilcloth. Could this be meat from the boar Rabbie had killed only a short time ago? Isobel said Rabbie loved her. Could it be true?

She glanced at Fin. He felt her gaze and turned his face away to shove a loaf of bread into an already-full pack.

Isobel had been the one to tell Catriona where they were going. Lady Ogilvie had asked them to leave the castle as soon as possible and take the Honours of Scotland with them. Keeping the ancient regalia out of the hands of the English was paramount. Foreigners could not take something that the Scottish people valued so highly. It was a part of their heritage that they held dear. The Grahams had to keep every piece safe.

Catriona glanced at the trunk housing the golden crown and its companion pieces. She had to ask.

"Will ye be searching for Rabbie still?" If his family planned to abandon him, Catriona would find him by herself. She had no skill with any weapons, but she would learn.

Fin scowled at her, his red brows puckering. "Of course we will. The Grahams take care of their own. Do ye ken our motto?"

She shook her head. The Dunns had no motto she knew of. Why had she never thought to ask Da? Now it was too late.

"*Ne oublie*. It means "Dinna forget," and so we won't forget about Rabbie. He's my brother. We will find him."

Before she had a chance to respond, Isobel came into the room. Her mouth was drawn into a grim line of determination. "Come with me, Cat. If ye are going to be a Graham, ye must dress like one."

71

"Yer Da said I can come with ye?" Catriona's voice was muffled as she pulled her kirtle over her head.

"Yes, ye must learn to be a falconer though."

"I will. I will." Off came Catriona's shoes and stockings.

"I may have lost my mamm, but I've gained a sister."

Catriona glanced at her companion and sat on the bed with a thump. Isobel gave her a sad smile. She returned it in kind. "Aye, I feel the same way."

Minutes later, Catriona had shed her dress and donned beeches, a loose-fitting linen shirt, stockings, boots, and a long tunic that was belted at the waist. Now she and Isobel were dressed in the same manner. For that matter, she wore what Fin and Rabbie usually wore. She wondered what Da would say seeing his daughter dressed as a man. She expected he would be amused and perhaps even proud that she would be taking part in this mission.

Catriona walked on wobbly legs around Isobel's room. "Having material on my legs is a bit strange. 'Tis rather freeing to be able to move so easily."

"I enjoy dressing this way. I find it much more liberating than skirts." Isobel smiled for the first time since the loss of her mother. "Why should the lads have all the fun?"

"It will take getting used to."

Isobel jumped up. "Time to go. We must get out of Dunnottar without being attacked.

Da has been talking to the men-at-arms; the only way out is by the sea."

Catriona gasped. "But, Belle, I cannae swim!"

"Och, don't be daft. We'll be in boats. No one in their right mind would swim the North Sea in the winter." Isobel sat on the bed and patted the spot beside her. "Come. Sit. We need to braid yer hair so the birds donna get their claws caught in it."

"But didna Fin let them all loose?"

"Aye. We will get them back. You'll see."

"All right then," Catriona sat while Isobel's nimble fingers wove the black strands in a long braid then wrapped it securely around her head.

With no flowing hair to deal with, Catriona's entire body and head felt lighter and freer than before. The physicals weights of clothing and hair were removed, leaving behind only the mental weight to burden her.

Everything she had known was now buried in the kirkyard. She stole a glance at Isobel from under her lashes. At some point, they would both take the time to properly mourn their lost parents.

Catriona stood and straightened her spine. "I'm ready to learn falconry, Belle, and to do whatever the Graham clan asks of me. I want to go find Rabbie right now and help keep the Honours away from the English.

Chapter 9

After packing what they needed, Boyd, in his paternal and authoritative way, insisted that everyone eat and take their rest. For the second night, Catriona shared a bed with Isobel. But this night, the house was gloomy and the sounds of quiet sobbing lasted for several hours before silence fell.

Someone shook her shoulder only a short time after she finally fell asleep. Her scratchy, irritated eyes focused on a face with the same handsome features and cheekbones as Rabbie, but with different coloring as befits a true redhead.

"Get up, both of ye. We're leaving."

Night still cloaked the castle. A few candles had been lit in the main room of the Graham house, casting their surroundings in a warm, cozy glow. One of the Dunnottar men-at-arms waited there, his face was an emotionless mask. A strange sense of anxiety and gloom hung over them all as they prepared to leave. Each member of the Graham clan would be carrying as much as possible in a sack that could be slung over one shoulder or carried on one's back.

One by one, they stepped out of the door and crept along the shadowy stone walls until they reached the north wing of the palace. Their escort knocked softy three times on the door, waited a beat, and knocked once more.

The door creaked open a crack, revealing a man holding a single candle. His eyes

74

darted to each person, then he nodded and eased the door open wide enough to allow them to come inside. This was all done without a word spoken.

Catriona followed the tiny point of light, walking behind Fin and Isobel. Her thoughts bounced around in her head, flitting from one topic to another. She pushed any thoughts of Da to one side for now. His passing was too raw, too painful, and too new to consider without becoming emotional, which she couldn't afford to do right now.

They walked through a portion of the palace that Rabbie had showed her only a few days before. Thick, plush carpeting lined the floor. Gleaming furniture made of rich woods stood about like sentinels. The frozen faces of Scottish royalty, some larger than life, hung on the walls. Elegant porcelain figurines stood on tabletops. Catriona was careful not to touch a single one. Life had seemed so full of promise and happiness when they had exclaimed over each item together. He had even put his hand on the small of her back to guide her through the halls.

Everything had changed so suddenly that her head was still spinning.

Boyd Graham was behind her this time; she could hear him breathing.

They turned to the right and entered an area of the palace that Rabbie had not shown her. Unfortunately, the passageway was so dark that she could tell little about their surroundings other than the floor became hard when the plush carpeting ended.

Within minutes, they stepped outside of the building. Cool air hit Catriona's face, and they passed through a large stone archway.

"This is the Water Gate," Isobel turned to whisper to her. "We're going down the cliffs now, so be careful where you step. Mist makes the stones slippery."

Boyd came up beside them. "Follow my children, Catriona. Step where they step and hold onto what they hold. They've experience with climbing and descending cliffs."

Catriona nodded, memories of Rabbie easily scaling the cliff in search of young falcons made this fact very believable.

A faint tinge of early gray dawn stained the sky, giving her just enough light to see Isobel and Fin in front of her. Cold wind bit into Catriona's face and froze her exposed hands. She was grateful now to be wearing breeches instead of a skirt that would have wrapped dangerously around her trembling legs.

"Don't look down at the water. Keep your eyes on me and the path."

The narrow passage down the cliffside alternated between stone steps and a rocky path. Catriona no longer used one hand to hold her pack and one hand for support, she held tight with both hands to any part of the cliff available. The weight of the pack threatened to pull her backwards as she pressed her body against the mountain face, clinging to the stones for dear life.

One step sideways and down, then another, and another. If she fell to her death, the sceptre in her pack would be lost in the

North Sea right along with her body. Of course, each one of them had part of the Honours hidden in their packs, so any one of them could be lost and lose the regalia forever.

Catriona thought this to be a brilliant plan, assuming they all made it through. If one member of their party was captured by the English, the remaining pieces of the regalia could be saved.

"I-is t-this truly the only way out of Dunnottar?" she gasped.

"Yes." Boyd's voice at her left was strong and calm. "English troops would surely kill us if they caught us going down the normal road. You're doing good, lassie. Before ye ken it, we'll be down. Cináed would be proud of his braw daughter. I ken it."

Catriona blinked away the sting of tears at the mention of her father. She pulled her face away from the cold, wet rock; straightened up; moved another step down; and readjusted her handhold. She would keep going, she would inch her way down to sea level, and she would help find Rabbie. After that, she had no idea what would happen.

* * *

How he managed to fall asleep hanging by his wrists, Rabbie had no idea. Nor did he know what had awakened him other than pain in his shoulders. His hands had long since gone numb.

His torturer lay on the ground, huddled under a blanket, next to a dying fire. A few coals glowed red against the dark earth.

Rabbie blinked and examined the rows and rows of white tents in the graying sky. No one moved. To his good fortune, the English army still slept.

It was now or never.

With one swift motion, he threw his head and shoulders to the right, which caused his body to twist around and face the tree. Using this momentum, he walked his bare feet up the tree trunk as his shoulder muscles screamed in protest. With extreme effort, he hooked first his left then his right leg over the branch. For a moment, he hung there with his legs higher than his head.

One breath, two, and …

Rabbie pulled his torso toward the branch with his legs and loosened the tension on the rope, which allowed him to jerk the rope closer to the end of the branch. He repeated this action and ignored the stars exploding in his vision.

As Rabbie got closer to the end, the branch got thinner and bent under his weight. Suddenly, he hit the ground. Landing on his back drove the air right out of his lungs. He struggled to pull oxygen into his body without making any noise to awaken his captor.

"Where the bloody 'ell do you think you're going?"

The English soldier loomed above him. In the early morning light, the man's angry expression seemed demonic.

Rabbie closed his eyes.

* * *

At the bottom of the cliff, the Grahams and Catriona shook out the stiffness of their bodies after the long descent. In front of them, the North Sea moved restlessly against the backdrop of a steel gray sky. The air smelled of salty seawater.

"Guid morning! What brings ye fine folks down this side o' the mountain?"

They all turned to see a great, shaggy-haired, bearded man striding out of a cave. A huge broadsword was clutched in one hand, belying the friendliness of his greeting.

"Has no one brought word of the siege on Dunnottar to ye, friend?" Boyd Graham put out one hand to greet the man and held the other hand out to one side, showing that he carried no weapons.

"Och, nae. How bad is it?"

Rabbie's father provided the man-at-arms with a brief description of the British attack but didn't mention their secret cargo. When asked why the Graham falconers were leaving when no one else had yet to attempt the difficult climb down, Boyd recounted the capture of his son and the deaths of Moira and Cináed.

"Ye can understand how we must find our Rabbie, we canna stay inside the protective walls doing nothing."

"Aye, come, we've a small boat ye can use to get ashore beyond the cliffs."

Isobel and Catriona were instructed to wait outside while the two Graham men followed the guard inside the cave. Both women moved closer to a small cook fire at the mouth of the cave and sat on rocks.

Even the little heat afforded by the dancing flames helped warm Catriona's frozen fingers, and she sighed.

"Rabbie really does love you."

Catriona lifted her head and met her new friend's steady blue eyes. Isobel's expression seemed to challenge Catriona to disagree.

"You and Rabbie are close then?"

"Aye, Fin and Rabbie are closer to each other, being boys...er...men and all. But I'm lucky to have brothers who treat me well and talk to me honestly."

"You are lucky, Isobel. I never had any brothers, sisters, or even cousins. My Mamm died when I was little, and my Da raised me..." Her throat thickened, but she kept going, "...and now he's gone too."

Isobel draped an arm around Catriona's shoulder and they pulled closer together.

"I'll be your sister, if you'd like. If Rabbie is truly sweet on you, maybe..."

Isobel's unspoken words though sent a jolt through Catriona. The possibility that she and Rabbie could be together was a truly happy prospect. She couldn't imagine leaving him behind to strike out on her own alone. Was this feeling love or just the need to fill the recent void in her life?

"Dinna fash yerself aboot it, Cat." Isobel must have read the uncertainty in her face. "If ye and Rabbie are meant to be together, God will see it done. Too much has happened to think on it now."

A large tear rolled down Isobel's freckled face. "Mamm—" she choked and couldn't continue.

Catriona's vision blurred with her own tears, and she hugged her new "sister" close as they both sobbed over their lost parents.

"Stop your weeping women, we've got to go."

Catriona looked up to see Fin glaring down at both of them; his eyes were suspiciously red-rimmed. She jumped up immediately, dashing away the wetness on her face with both hands. "The sooner we find Rabbie, the better."

How she wished he were here now. Having him take her in his arms and hold her would be heaven on earth. Catriona yearned to see his handsome face and smiling blue eyes. She hadn't known Rabbie Graham for very long, but she sincerely hoped she would get a chance to know him better.

The sun had risen in Aberdeenshire and burned off the gray clouds. They climbed into the small boat with their precious load.

Catriona sat in the middle of the boat and held on tightly to the side. She had never been in a boat before and decided it was not an enjoyable experience. Just a thin layer of wood stood between them and the dark water of the North Sea. Her knees shook and her whole body trembled. She couldn't swim, but she could pray, so she did.

As the two men took turns rowing their small party out of the protected cover and turned to the west, the light danced off restless waters making it sparkle. Catriona had to admit that it was pretty, but she was still very nervous.

She closed her burning eyes as the sea wind blew in her face. The misty air filled her lungs, and the little boat rocked and bobbed in the water. The day was shaping up to be cool but beautiful … a perfect day for a very important hunt.

Chapter 10

"Keep your eyes open for any signs of soldiers. We dinna want to be caught defenseless on open ground when we touch land." Boyd's voice was calm but firm.

He had every reason to worry. They didn't know exactly where the English camp lay. Catriona had a good idea where they had been located when she and Rabbie first found them, but they could have moved by now.

Was Rabbie with them? Was he even alive? Catriona bit her lip and pushed her hands deep into the pockets of her coat to keep from fidgeting, then had pull them back out again to brace herself as the boat rocked gently from side to side. She turned to Isobel.

"Your Da said that Rabbie's falcon would find him. But how are we going to find his falcon and follow it? You and Fin let them all go back to the wilderness."

Isobel didn't take her eyes off the approaching shoreline. "Yes, we did set them all loose. Some will return when we call. Others will never come back. Rabbie's Brisda always came back to him. We hope she will come to us and then lead us to him."

Fin gave a final heave with the oars and the boat scraped along the small rocky beach. He jumped out and pulled the boat onto land. Giving each of them a hand, he and his father helped them out and handed them their packs.

After they dragged the boat a short distance, the four covered it with seaweed and brush to hide it. Any Dunnottar resident would know they could find a boat on this beach and use it to get to the castle's sea gate.

They all donned their packs and struck off, heading toward the tree line.

They hadn't gone far when they reached a small clearing in the scrubby forest that sprang up all around the beach area.

"Let's have a go at it here." Boyd Graham motioned for them to drop their packs.

Catriona sat on a damp log to watch. Isobel, Fin, and Boyd stood a short distance away from each other on the rocky ground. Tufts of grass sprang out of the earth here and there under their feet.

It was time to get the falcons back. Boyd, the Grand Falcon, tried first. Pressing his lips together, he let out a piercing series of clipped sounds. The calls sounded unusual to Catriona's ears, but after a few minutes of this, a large bird appeared and circled overhead. Then a second dark-winged shape joined the first as they soared and dipped in the clear blue sky. Their majestic air dance made Catriona's throat inexplicably tighten.

Boyd donned the long, leather gauntlet and took a piece of meat out of his pack. Holding his fist up in the air, he continued the calls. After a few minutes, a big bird flew close to Catriona's head. The wind rustled her hair as a dark blur shot past her and landed on Boyd's fist. He fed it the meat he had and fished inside his pouch for another morsel.

The magnificent peregrine falcon had mostly gray feathers with some brown and white accents on her wings. The bird looked familiar.

"Look, Cat. Brisda came back first! It's Rabbie's falcon!" Isobel's face lit up with her excitement.

Catriona came close to look at the falcon a bit closer. The creature sat tall on Boyd's glove, her black eyes flicked around at her surroundings. "Hello, Brisda, remember me? Can you help find Rabbie, Brisda?" The bird just blinked in response.

Catriona helped Fin assemble the cadge perches and pieces he had carried down the cliffside in his pack. Boyd transferred Brisda from his fist to a perch and tied the bird's leather jesses to a perch.

"Please give her a bit more food, but not too much or she won't want to fly. Wear a glove. Remember, this is still a wild animal," Boyd advised.

Catriona donned a leather glove and offered the falcon three more pieces of meat with her protected hand.

The bird gobbled up the meat immediately, and Catriona carefully lowered the hood over her head, fully expecting the falcon to pull away or try to avoid the hood. But it was as if the hawk was expecting to be hooded; she allowed Catriona to place it on her little head and didn't try to bite the leather. Finishing this task, Catriona returned to watch the falconers at work.

Isobel whistled and whistled, but no majestic falcon soared down from the blue sky to her glove.

Her brother stood several paces away, held up his glove with a piece of meat and whistled too. Everyone tilted their heads to scan above the treetops. Nothing. Fin whistled three more times and finally a speck appeared. Closer and closer, the speck resolved into a bird, and finally, his falcon Grizel landed on his fist with a final flap of wings.

Catriona was fascinated as she watched Boyd successfully call two more of their flock to his fist, but his personal hawk and Isobel's were not among those recovered.

With at least some of their hunting birds back, the Graham men decided to get some food before continuing their journey. Isobel and Catriona were left to set up a camp of sorts and to find some fresh water.

They quickly located a nearby stream and filled their skin pouches. Coming back to the camp, Catriona poured some water from her pouch into a small tin cup, placed it near Brisda's perch, and then removed the hood so the bird could drink. They had not taken Rabbie's hawk hunting so that she would be rested and ready to search for her master. The peregrine fixed bright black eyes on Catriona and watched her every move.

"Ye've got to find Rabbie tomorrow, Brisda," she whispered to the bird, "or so help me, I will pluck out your tail feathers."

"Catriona!" Isobel chuckled as she walked up beside her. "Would you really do that to Rabbie's falcon?"

Blood rushed to Catriona's face. Isobel's hearing was excellent. "No, I suppose I wouldn't do that. After all, it is a wild creature with no real idea of our wants and desires."

Isobel reached out and stroked Brisda's breast feathers with her fingertips. "There's a bonnie wee hawk," she cooed then turned to Catriona. "Touch her like I did, Cat. Ye need to be more comfortable with the beasties."

Catriona did as she was asked but remained ready to pull her hand away if the bird pecked at her. Brisda's pretty plumage was soft and clean, and Catriona could feel the springy muscles and hard bones lurking under the surface.

"Dinnae look straight into her eyes, Cat. 'Twill be seen as aggression on yer part."

"Oh!" She dropped her gaze to the powerful claws. With those sharp claws and beak, the bird could inflict painful injuries to anyone. Catriona had no desire to invoke the hawk's ire.

Men's voices, talking in low tones, caught her attention. Fin and Boyd had returned. Perhaps they'd be ready to search for Rabbie soon.

* * *

"Just tell me where the Honours of Scotland are located, and maybe I'll let you live. Why should you care about some rich man's crown? You aren't a rich man are you? No, you aren't. They wouldn't care about you. So talk. The vultures are circling to pick your bones clean." The burly soldier spat the words into Rabbie's face in a cloud of foul-smelling breath. Rabbie's eyes watered at the stench, but he didn't speak. Since his escape attempt, he'd been hung up by his wrists again and whipped on his bare back with a horsewhip.

The man's thick fingers dug into Rabbie's lower jaw as his head was forced back until he saw the sky. Sure enough, a single bird circled overhead. But Rabbie knew instantly that this was no vulture; it was a falcon, a peregrine falcon to be exact.

A flicker of hope sparked in his heart.

A second red-coated soldier walked up just then, eying Rabbie with obvious distaste. "Longbottom, we're moving out. Leave him there. Time to kill his people."

His torturer hesitated, stopping in front of Rabbie, who cracked his eyes open just a bit to see what the man would do.

"It would be more merciful if I were to bury my knife in your heart." He jerked his head toward a tree across from where Rabbie hung. "But letting the vulture slowly pick you apart piece by piece, making you linger and suffer is more my style." Throwing back his head, he laughed nastily, kicked dirt over the cook fire, picked up his coat, and walked away to join the others.

No vulture perched in that tree.

A beautiful, sleek bird with brown, gray, and white feathers fixed shiny black eyes on Rabbie.

Brisda had found him.

* * *

"How do we know she is leading us to Rabbie? Maybe she is just flying around." Catriona accepted Fin's hand to climb onto a rock and jump over a small running brook.

He tipped back his head and pushed a lock of unruly red hair out of his face.

Silhouetted against the blue afternoon sky, the falcon flew in wide, sweeping circles that progressed ever westward.

"We don't really know, but we've little choice but to try. Our kinsmen are trapped in Dunnottar and canna help us. Da and I have talked about the whole situation. Once we find Rabbie, we must hide the Honours in a safe place. We just havena figured out where that safe place would be.

Catriona pushed a stay strand of hair out of her face and tucked it back into her braid. The day that had started out sunny had turned icy and gray. Clouds hung low in the sky, heavy with impending snow. She could smell it coming.

A sense of urgency in the group quickened their pace. Catriona developed a crick in her neck from looking up for the falcon as they hurried faster through the trees, stirring up the scent of pine needles and rotting leaves.

Finally, Brisda seemed to stop her forward progression. The falcon rose up into the air above the treetops then dropped abruptly out of sight, only to reappear seconds later to repeat the motion.

Fin began to run, leaving Isobel, Catriona, and Boyd to follow as quickly as they could.

Large, wet snowflakes drifted lazily down to melt on Catriona's nose and cheeks. She pulled her woolen scarf up over her hair without breaking stride. Rabbie had to be close now.

A shout broke the sound of their panting breaths.

"Fin's found him!" Isobel's excitement infected them all, and they sprinted forward over a small rise.

Catriona spotted Brisda perched high in a pine tree overlooking the events unfolding below.

Two men were huddled together on the ground. Fin had apparently cut the rope that now dangled from a branch.

"Rabbie!" Catriona couldn't help but cry out when she saw him lying half in his brother's lap. Fin used his *sgian dubh* to deftly removed the rope binding Rabbie's wrists.

"His hands!" Get the blood into his hands!" Fin cried.

Dropping to her knees in the carpet of pine needles, Catriona took one ice-cold hand in hers and rubbed. Isobel copied her actions.

Rabbie's face contorted with pain and he moaned softly as they worked.

Catriona stole a quick, anxious look at Rabbie. His lower lip was swollen to twice its size and one eye had swelled shut. Dirt and blood smeared his naked upper body.

Boyd appeared with a blanket and wrapped it around his shivering son. "I'll get a fire going," he murmured to no one in particular.

Catriona concentrated on moving the blood back into Rabbie's long, swollen fingers. She watched them go from white to pink and purple. *God, please dinna let him lose his hands.*

"H-hallo, Catriona." Rabbie offered her a shaky smile as she continued to work on his hands.

"Hallo yerself, Rabbie Graham. Looks like ye've been badly used."

"Aye." He gasped and arched his back when Fin shifted under him to move away.

"Och, man, what did the bastards do to you?" Fin leaned over him to pull away the blanket and look at Rabbie's back. He snorted an angry Scottish noise. "They whipped you, the dirty scum!"

"No!" Isobel whispered. Tear sslipped down her face, but she kept rubbing his fingers.

"Oh, Rabbie!" Catriona pulled his swollen hand up and held it to her cheek. She fought to control her own tears.

This time Rabbie snorted. "No waterworks, you two. I'm still alive." He swiveled toward his father, who had gotten a nice fire started. "Have ye got any food, Da? And where is Mamm?"

The ever-present sorrow on Boyd Graham's face deepened. Catriona knew he had to tell his oldest son the bad news.

"Let's get some food into you and clean ye up first, Rabbie lad. The tale can wait."

Rabbie's good eye widened. He pulled his hands free and leaped to his feet. He stood, swaying slightly, in front of his father.

"Da, I've abided this long, I believe I can go longer. Tell me what I need to ken."

Catriona wanted to jump up and wrap Rabbie in her arms but knew he wouldn't want it just now. Emotions flickered across Boyd's face—hesitation, acceptance, sorrow, and finally pride for the exhausted, injured man in front of him.

"Aye, I will tell you now, son. Sit, eat, and let Catriona tend to yer back while I do."

So, Boyd related the entire story, while Isobel sniffed and turned the skewered rabbit over the fire.

Catriona tried not to sob aloud as she washed and applied ointment and bandages to Rabbie's back then helped him into a clean shirt and coat.

Fin fed and hooded the falcons. They had all flown free during the search for Rabbie and now came back to roost.

Light snow continued to fall as darkness crept in, stealing all color from their surroundings.

Rabbie's stark white face sagged with weariness and sorrow. "Mamm is gone? Catriona's Da too?"

Boyd nodded.

His son's dark head dropped into his swollen hands. "What now? Will we be leaving Dunnottar to the English?"

Boyd sat down on a log next to Rabbie. "We've been given a sacred mission to accomplish. Lady Ogilvie has entrusted the

Graham falconers with the safety of the Scottish regalia. This is a grand and valuable symbol of our heritage and pride. It has been used to coronate monarchs from Queen Mary the First in 1543 to our own Charles the Second. We canna go back to Dunnottar until the regalia is securely hidden away from the English."

"The Dunnottar men-at-arms will defend the castle." Isobel's declaration held more confidence than Catriona felt.

Catriona stood next to Rabbie with one hand resting lightly on his shoulder. "How did the Honours come to be at Dunnottar?" There was so much Catriona didn't know. She had been raised to be a baker and a wife, nothing more. Da had taught her to read and write recipes for the different types of breads. She could keep records of their money and sales, but she had never read a book like the fine, leather-bound volumes Rabbie had shown her in the palace.

Rabbie raised his head. Mild surprise, but not censure showed on his face. Heat rushed up Catriona's neck at her lack of knowledge. He must have sensed her discomfort for he patted the stone beside him, offering her a seat.

She sat, took his swollen right hand, and gently massaged the stiff fingers. He sighed and relaxed into her as his father spoke.

"After the English Parliament had Charles the First executed, Oliver Cromwell, the so-called Lord Protector, ordered the regalia to be melted down. As soon as Charles the Second was coronated, the Honours were sent secretly to Dunnottar, probably because 'tis easily defended with the castle located on the cliff."

"Where will we be taking the regalia, Da?" Rabbie's voice had grown slow and sleepy.

"Eat," Catriona whispered and offered him a piece of cooked meat on a stick.

Rabbie obligingly opened his mouth for the morsel and took it. He flexed his fingers slightly to work them as he chewed, but Catriona could see the action pained him. She continued to hold the food and drink to his mouth for him.

"I've nae idea, son."

After a few minutes, Fin joined them at the fireside, shaking snow off his head and shoulders. "Isobel and I have gathered branches for a shelter and could use yer help, Da."

Catriona stood. "I can help."

But Isobel came up and put a hand on her shoulder and spoke softly into her ear. "Please Cat, stay with Rabbie. He needs you here. He shouldna be left alone right now."

Rabbie had stopped speaking and stared into the fire with haunted eyes.

Catriona nodded and sat beside him again.

The rest of the Graham family disappeared into the darkness and swirling snow beyond the fire's reach.

"Rest yer head, Rabbie." Catriona wrapped an arm around his shoulders and pulled him to her. Letting out another long sigh, Rabbie put his head in her lap. He let her comfort him and stroke his cheek until his eyes closed.

"I thank God above we've found ye," Catriona said quietly to the sleeping man. "I've no one else in the world now."

Chapter 11

Rabbie woke some time during the night. At first, he had no inkling of where he was, or the identity of these people lying next to him, lined up like birds on a branch. Gradually, he remembered that he had been rescued, and his memories returned. His family and Catriona Dunn, the baker's daughter, had come to rescue him. When he smiled at the thought of being valued enough to be saved, his battered face ached with the motion.

Then he remembered that Mamm was dead and the smile dissolved. His insides felt strangely constricted. Dear little Mamm with her fiery spirit and kind brown eyes; she was bigger than life. How could she be gone? He hadna even said goodbye.

His throat tightened, but he controlled himself. *A grown man canna cry.*

Slowly and painfully, he rolled away from the sleeping forms of the others. He opened his mouth to gulp the cold air like a fish. Deep breaths to stop the weeping did not work completely, and he stifled another sob.

Mamm. Oh Mamm.

A small hand stroked his hair. She didn't say a word, but Rabbie knew it was Catriona who lay behind him. His heart broke for her as well. She had lost her only family. Rabbie had really liked Cináed Dunn. He wondered how Catriona had come to be with the Graham family. Why had she not stayed behind in the relative safety of Dunnottar Castle?

He was glad of her presence, though. Something about the black-haired beauty called to his soul … and it was not just her appearance. There was more to Catriona. For those few times when he was with her, his heart soared and his spirit was peaceful, even if his body was not. Despite the injuries he'd suffered, the thought of Catriona sent blood rushing to his masculine parts. This time he had to suppress a moan of desire. Guilt washed over him. How could he be thinking of such pleasures when people had died?

Then her fingers moved from his hair, slid down his shoulder, and came to rest on his hip, a warm spot that grounded him in this world. When she didn't move her fingers further, he gradually relaxed and let exhaustion take over.

"Och, Rabbie, yer old Da is sorry to wake ye, but the snow is falling fast and we must be on our way."

Snow? Rabbie scrambled stiffly to his feet, scrubbing the melted snow over his face as he squinted at the sky then met his father's gaze.

"Sorry, Da." A huge yawn took his breath away.

"Nae apologies, son. Ye've been through a hard time and need rest, but we cannae linger here. The snow and the English are both against us."

Everyone stood around a hissing campfire where a skinned rabbit roasted on a skewer. Isobel handed Rabbie a cup of hot tea. He sipped it, tasting the willow bark she'd added to reduce swelling and pain.

"How are you today?" His sister searched his face for a moment then glanced away when the fire sizzled louder under the onslaught of snow and animal fat.

"Fair." He too stared at the fire, afraid to look at Catriona or the others for fear they'd read his raw emotions too plainly.

"Meat's almost done," Fin said and gave him a weak smile.

Rabbie nodded. "I'll not break, ye ken. You can all act normal like."

He had given them permission to relax, and puffs of air were expelled by all in little clouds of steam in the cold air.

"Where are we going?" he asked no one in particular, but Catriona answered.

"I realized where we are this morning in the daylight, and we're not far from my house. We can all stay there … to rest up and let this storm pass."

Rabbie heard the excitement in her voice at the prospect of going home. Her pleasure made him feel happier as well.

"Aye, 'tis a good idea at that. Thank ye, Cat."

A small smile lifted her pretty mouth, and she nodded.

A blast of wind and pelting snowflakes had each of them pulling up hoods, donning hats, or wrapping scarves around their heads and faces. Rabbie gave silent thanks to the Heavenly Father that his family had rescued him before the snow came.

"Let's eat." Da reached for the skewer and pulled the roasted meat off the fire.

* * *

Catriona walked behind Rabbie to make sure he kept putting one foot in front of the other. Shortly after setting out, he was panting for breath as he struggled to plow through the deepening snow behind his brother.

"Is that yer wee house, Catriona?" Fin pointed straight ahead.

Catriona had to squint to see beyond the curtain of falling snow. The dark outlines of a small, thatched-roof stone cottage and their smaller bakehouse lay a short distance ahead.

"Yes!" she cried out and took off running as best she could through the snow. "I'm home! I'm home!"

She passed everyone and took the lead, joyfully bounding toward the door. "Da, I'm home! Where are ye?"

Suddenly someone grabbed her arm and pulled her to a stop. "Let me go, Rabbie! I'm going to see—"

He yanked her around to face him with strength she didn't think possible. "Nae, Cat. Your Da insna here. Remember?"

Realization of the truth hit her like a physical blow, and her knees buckled. Rabbie tried to hold her up, but he had lost too much. They both went down in the snow.

Icy wetness trailed down her cheeks as she sobbed.

"Shh, Cat. Shh, *mo leannan*." Rabbie wrapped both arms around her. Holding her

DIANE WYLIE

close, he rocked her like a child. "Dinna fash
yerself, the Grahams will care for you now."

He didn't know, didn't understand that
she was not crying for herself or her future,
she was crying for her lost father. The father
who raised her after her mother died; the
father who taught her how to bake. Deep
inside of her, a little voice struggled to be
heard … the voice that told her she could
bake bread and rolls and make her own way
in the world. But the overwhelming loss of
her father, her only family, tamped down that
voice, and she allowed Rabbie's words to
provide comfort to her wounded soul.

"Come." Boyd and Isobel got on either
side and pulled both to their feet. Fin's hands
were full as he was carrying the cadge
perches where the four falcons sat hooded
and silent.

With Isobel helping her and Boyd
helping Rabbie, they finally made it to the
front door. Catriona took off her glove and
felt under a square brown stone; the key was
still there! Her frozen, trembling hands gave
her a bit of trouble, but she got the lock open,
and they all stumbled inside the cottage.

* * *

Rabbie sank into a chair and watched
Catriona with open concern. Had she just
forgotten her father's death in the excitement
of the moment or had her mind decided to
ignore the facts? He'd have to keep an eye on
the lassie…his lassie. For that is how he
thought of her now, as his. He'd nothing on
which to base this conclusion, this was just

the way he felt. If she was here now, with the Graham family, it was meant to be.

Her pale face drooped with sadness. But as he watched her take off her coat and hang it on a peg, a slow metamorphosis seemed to take place. Her green eyes flicked around the room, touching on each one of the Grahams and on the simple furnishings of her home. The earlier anguish on her face eased, her chin lifted just a bit, and she let out a shuddering breath. Catriona seemed to mentally shake off her gloom, the way the falcons shake then settle their feathers when they rouse themselves.

In minutes, she had Rabbie's father building a fire, set Fin and Isobel to devising a place inside for the falcons, and had made Rabbie move to her father's big chair near the hearth.

Catriona paused in front of Rabbie and took his still-swollen hands in hers. Rubbing and massaging, she worked on both hands for several minutes until he could flex his fingers again.

Rabbie unclenched his jaw as the pain from her ministrations began to fade. "Thank ye, Catriona."

"Keep moving them, Rabbie," she said softly. "Before ye ken it, they'll be back to normal."

He nodded and curled his fingers into a poor semblance of a fist then relaxed. Gazing around the cottage as he worked, he was impressed. It was a good-sized, solid structure made of local stone. A raised hearth sat in the middle of the room, and smoke was vented through the thatched roof.

"Did Cináed build this place? Wonderful construction, what with the fireplace in the middle o' the room. Verra smart." Boyd smiled at Catriona as he laid the fire.

"Aye, Da built it for my mother, and he built a separate building just for baking. Mamm had her kitchen in here, and Da did his baking in the bakehouse." She visibly blinked back tears and swallowed hard. "Mr. Graham, you and Fin can use my Da's bedroom over there." She pointed to a darkened doorway to Rabbie's left. Then she glanced at Rabbie and his father with an expression of uncertainty and furrowed brow. "I dinna ken where the rest of us should sleep. We've only my bed there ..." She pointed to a nice-sized wood frame bed peeking out from behind a blanket partition. "... and a cot we use for visitors."

A chill struck Rabbie hard, and he shivered despite the roaring fire in front of him. "If ye dinnae mind, I'd like to sleep close to the fire. It seems the cold has seeped into my bones."

Isobel and Fin came over to join the conversation.

"I took a look in your father's room, Catriona. The bed is big enough for me to sleep there with Da and Fin. That way, you can sleep in your own bed and we can set up the cot for Rabbie." Isobel grinned at them all, obviously pleased with her pronouncement.

Catriona nodded and led Fin away to fetch the cot. Rabbie watched her hips swaying as she walked away. Catriona in man's breeches was a sight to behold. All of the pain from his injuries seemed to disappear, and his fingers itched to be wrapped around that shapely bum.

Several strands of wavy dark hair had come loose from their braids and hung down her back. He would love to feel the softness of those tresses against his cheek.

His attention jerked back to his own discomforts as another chill struck, making his teeth chatter. The wind howled outside the cottage as if to chill him further. He wrapped both arms around himself to try to stop the vibrations running through him.

Isobel bent to peer into his face. With effort, he attempted to smile reassuringly, but his mouth didn't seem to obey him. She put a hand to his forehead just like their Mamm did when they were little children.

"Fever." Her statement made Da's eyes widen.

"No, Belle. I'm just cold from our trip." Rabbie accepted a blanket his father handed him. But two minutes later, he pushed it off. Then he stood, pulled off his heavy coat, and stumbled toward the door. Yanking open the heavy door, he sighed and sagged against the doorframe when frigid air blasted into his burning face.

"Come, son." Da took his shoulders, gently pulled him away from the door, and closed it. "No need to freeze us all."

* * *

"What's the matter?" Catriona and Fin had come back with the cot to see Boyd leading his son away from the door. "Were you leaving, Rabbie?"

She hoped the hurt and disappointment didn't show in her voice. Why would he leave in the middle of a blizzard?

He turned toward her, shrugging off his father's supporting arm. "No, I'm not leaving, Catriona, I just needed some cool air."

The corners of his mouth lifted as he attempted a smile. He extended a hand, so she took it. His fingers were still slightly swollen from the rope, and raw marks showed on his wrist, reminding Catriona of what he had endured.

"Fin and I have set up the cot for ye near the fire. Come."

When he didn't move, she jerked to a surprised stop and turned around, still holding his hand.

"Could we move it away from the hearth? I'm verra hot now."

Isobel came up beside him. "Rabbie's feverish, Cat."

"Just a wee bit. I'm not sick."

The stubborn Scotsman came out in his voice, but Catriona was too tired to play games with this man.

"Listen to me, Robert Graham, you may be no relation of mine, but I willna put up with foolishness in my house." Catriona yanked him toward the cot. "Ye'll let us take care of you and ye'll do it now!"

Despite a string of Gaelic curses from Rabbie, she and Isobel took matters into their own hands and stripped Rabbie down to his underthings in front of the fire to smothered chuckles from Boyd and Fin.

"You are making things worse. Da and Fin, ye can take care of food for the falcons and for us while we tend to our brother?" Isobel pointed a finger toward the birds, giving her menfolk a stern scowl.

"If I didna feel so bad, I wouldna let you treat me like t-this." His teeth started to chatter as he spoke, and he swayed just a bit.

"Sit down before ye fall." Catriona took hold of his bare arm and urged him to sit on the cot. Before letting go, she indulged in a quick caress, enjoying the smooth muscle under his skin.

Then Isobel and Catriona cleaned and redressed Rabbie's wounds as he lay on his belly. By the time they finished, he was breathing regularly, sound asleep.

"Come, Catriona, we've food prepared for you." Boyd stood beside the cot, a tender expression on his face, so much like his sons, still handsome but aged a bit.

She glanced at Rabbie, reluctant to leave his side.

"He'll bide, lass. You'll only be a few feet away," Boyd said.

With a nod, she rose from the chair and followed him to the table where a bowl of rabbit stew, prepared by the ever-talented Graham men, sat waiting for her.

They ate in silence, each with their own thoughts.

Catriona finished quickly then returned to sit on one of the heavy wooden chairs near

Rabbie once more. A big stack of wood had been piled nearby to dry for later use.

All of the Grahams but Rabbie still sat at the table. They had begun to talk in hushed tones, either to keep from disturbing Rabbie or to keep her from overhearing. She wasn't sure, nor did she care. Rabbie was her only concern now.

The sound of a chair scraping back across the hard-packed dirt floor a few minutes later caught Catriona's attention. She looked up to see Fin approaching.

Tall, like the other Grahams, Fin had a ruddier complexion than his brother, as befits a redhead, and the firelight made him appear even warmer.

He went down on his haunches beside her. "How is he doing?" He tilted his head toward his brother, his expression filled with concern.

"Nothing to do but wait for the fever to leave. You all may as well go to sleep. I'll be nearby in case he needs something."

Fin nodded. "Aye, if it willna bother you, I'll be taking your pack with the sceptre and hiding it under the bed. We've tried to hide each piece of the Honours in a different place."

Catriona jerked her gaze away from Rabbie to Fin so fast that her neck bones creaked. "Have you reason to fear we'll be robbed?"

"Yes." He stood again. "Well, guid night to ye then."

She gaped at Fin as he casually beckoned to the others, picked up the pack she had carried down the cliffside, and they all disappeared into Da's bedroom.

Chapter 12

The rise and fall in volume of a
conversation woke Catriona. For a few
minutes, she lay in bed wondering why she
had slept fully clothed instead of donning her
usual nightgown. Then she remembered
yesterday's horror and last night's vigil with
a sick Rabbie Graham. Desolation filled her
heart. Da was gone. Dunnottar was under
siege. There was no need to get up and bake
bread. Even Roger the donkey was gone, lost.

*What are those falconers discussing so
urgently? Oh, yes, I have birds in my house too,
leaving their droppings on the floor.*

She sat up abruptly and glanced toward
the center of the room, but the partition
blocked her view. Had something happened
to Rabbie? He had experienced a bad night
with alternating fever and chills.

Throwing off the blankets, she proceeded
to yank on her stockings. She thought about
how much she liked wearing breeches, but
she would no longer need to dress that way.
Luckily, today's list of things to do did not
include climbing down a cliff, so she pulled
on a blouse, skirt, and her usual shoes then
emerged from her sleeping area.

Rabbie appeared to be sleeping in the
glow of a full roaring fire that someone had
replenished. He was still alive then. She
sighed with relief. The wind seemed to have
stopped its fierce assault on the little stone

cottage, so other noises became more prominent.

She walked toward the people gathered at the small wooden table. It looked as though Isobel had found the makings for a breakfast of porridge and bread.

The redheads greeted her with small smiles, puffy red-rimmed eyes, and hushed tones. Everyone was grieving.

"Guid morning, Cat. Would you like to eat?" Isobel had already picked up a bowl and headed toward the pot of porridge.

"Aye." Catriona sat and gratefully accepted a cup of meade from Fin. Isobel returned with the food seconds later. "What are you discussing, if ye dinna mind my asking?" Catriona spooned a bite of the hot cereal in her mouth then sighed. "Wonderful."

"Rabbie and the Honours," Fin said quietly with a glance at his sleeping brother.

"Did you come to some conclusion?" Catriona pulled off a piece of bread, popped it in her mouth, and chewed. It was a few days old and stale, but a little ale soon washed it down.

"He's not fit to travel, and we must be away today." Boyd reached out and put his hand on her arm as he spoke.

A wave of panic swept over Catriona. They were going to leave her here all alone! She had thought they would all stay here for the winter at least. In fact, the Grahams could live here if they wished.

When she softly told them this, Boyd patted her arm, just as her Da would when he wanted to placate her.

"'Tis sorry I am, lassie, but Lady Ogilvie entrusted us to protect the Honours, so we must get far away with them." Boyd's eyes, blue like Rabbie's, were full of sympathy. "We would take ye with us, if you desired to come but for Rabbie. I ken this is asking the moon, but would you stay and care for the lad until he is able to travel?"

Stunned at this turn of events, Catriona just stared at him. *Stay here? Just the two of them? Alone?*

Isobel met her gaze. She knew what had Catriona worried. "We ken it's improper for ye to live together here alone, so I have an idea. Rabbie loves ye. He told me so. Would you consider handfasting with him?"

"If you were married, it wouldna be improper for you and Rabbie to live here." Fin put in his opinion and nodded, his eyebrow raised in question."

"But—"

Boyd patted her hand again. "Ye've not got to answer now; ye've a few hours to decide while we prepare to leave. Fin and I are taking the birds out to hunt so we can have meat to take with us, and some to leave for you.

Catriona swallowed a lump of porridge and pushed the bowl away. Her hunger had vanished in a deluge of churning emotions.

* * *

Whose fat fingers are these? Rabbie didn't know, but he used them to push away the bowl. Someone was trying to make him eat nasty, lumpy porridge. He had always hated the stuff, and whenever it was served, Fin used the opportunity to mock him as less of a Scotsman.

Shoving off the smothering blankets, Rabbie sat up. His head spun as if he had drunk too much ale, but he had to get away from the fire. Too hot! He was cooking alive!

"You have to eat, Rabbie." Isobel sat beside him, holding the spoon out and waving it around. The gob of sticky cereal didn't fall off.

What a demanding sister. But this was just a dream. No one *had* to eat in a dream.

Rabbie knew it had to be a dream because he only wore underclothes, which was highly improper in the presence of a lady such as the baker's daughter.

He hauled himself to his feet. Belle jumped up faster and blocked his way.

"Move, Belle." But rather than wait for her to move, he stumbled around her. The door wasn't too far; this cottage was small. Vaguely, he wondered who lived here.

Then, there she was!

The baker's daughter, Catriona, with her dark hair down around her shoulders and her green eyes flashing a challenge, stood facing him with her back against the door.

Why were these women bothering him in his sleep? Can ye not do as you please in dreams? Rabbie just wanted to go lie down in the snow … white, fluffy, cool, clean snow.

"Not you too! Catriona, *mo leannan*, canna a man go outside to relieve himself?"

111

He braced his palms on the door above her shoulders so that her head was between his arms.

"Och, aye. But you cannae go outside in just yer under britches. You'll get sicker," she declared and crossed her arms over her beautiful chest.

Bending his head, Rabbie peered down at himself. He was almost naked. "Dinna fash yerself, I'm fine. I never get sick."

When he lifted his head again, he found himself gazing into the most beautiful set of green eyes he had ever seen. One of her perfect pink lips was caught between perfect white teeth. As she opened her mouth to speak again, Rabbie leaned in and claimed those lips with his. At first, she froze like a statue, and then she relaxed, so he stepped closer and eased his body against her while continuing to deepen the kiss. She tasted of porridge, but he didn't mind it on her.

He had to hold her. There were no consequences in dreams, and his father would never know. This was his dream, his business. So he slid his hands to her shoulders and pulled Catriona into his chest. Her blouse was soft against his skin. Next, he splayed his fingers through her silky hair and let the strands run through them like water.

His blood roared in his ears, and he was deaf to everything and blind to everyone but Catriona.

Rabbie grinned as her arms came up to drape around his neck, but the second she touched him, she gasped and jumped back.

"Rabbie, yer flaming like a hot oven!"

Her mouth moved, but he didn't understand her words. But he did know that she ruined his dream just when he was planning to taste her breasts. He scowled. If he couldn't kiss her, he would have his snow.

Rabbie stepped past her, yanked open the door, and tumbled out into the snow face first.

* * *

"I told ye he loves you, Cat."

Catriona didn't acknowledge Isobel's crow of triumph. "Just get his other arm. He's burning up and he's verra heavy." She plucked one of Rabbie's bare arms out of the snow where he lay, either asleep or unconscious. "His bandages are getting wet."

"So are his undergarments."

Isobel had hold of his other arm now. They heaved him around and dragged him back inside, but didn't have the strength to get him back on the cot.

"Now what shall we do with him?"

"We can't do anything but dry him off and wait for Da and Fin."

Isobel and Catriona both stared down at the half-naked man on the straw-covered floor.

Catriona knelt beside Rabbie and put a hand on his shoulder. "He was too hot a few minutes ago, but he feels a wee bit cooler now." She grabbed a blanket and began to dry off his face and body with Isobel's help. By the time they finished, the other two falconers came in, stomping the snow off their boots.

"What happened here?" Boyd stopped beside the women, who were both staring down at Rabbie again.

"He got out of bed and attacked Catriona." Isobel grinned and gave her a wink.

"Nay! He didna attack me!" Catriona glared at her friend.

"What did he do then?" Fin came up beside her, still holding a hooded falcon on his glove.

They all turned their gazes to Catriona. Heat rushed to her face. "He-he, um, well, he just kissed me is all."

Boyd let out a breath. "He must handfast w' you now, no question." Then he raised a ruddy eyebrow. "Why is he on the floor? Did ye bash him on the haid?"

"Nay, he went outside and fell asleep in the snow, so we dragged his carcass back inside." Isobel reached out her foot and nudged her fallen brother. He didn't stir.

Boyd's mouth flattened to a grim line, and he turned to his conscious children. "Get Rabbie up and dressed. Slap him if need be. We've nae time to waste. We're witnessing this ceremony now and leaving with the Honours. Fin saw a few English soldiers nearby. We must be away and canna wait for a sick man, even if it is our Rabbie."

Chapter 13

One minute Rabbie was sleeping peacefully for the first time in days, and the next minute Fin and Isobel were shaking him awake and pulling him up.

"W-what do ye want?" Rabbie stood swaying on his feet and feeling quite grumpy. His back ached relentlessly, he couldn't see that well out of one swollen eye, his hands throbbed, and he felt plainly unwell.

"You're getting married." Fin took his arm and began propelling him toward the door to someone's bedroom.

"Now? Why? Who am I marrying?" He tried to stop, but Isobel put her palms on his flayed back and pushed. "Oww. Yer cruel, Belle."

She laughed. "Aye, you're getting married now because you kissed Catriona, and we canna take ye with us."

"Och, I wasna dreaming then?"

"No. Get yer arse moving. Ye've got to dress. Da said we are to help you."

"Where is it you're going, and why can I not come?" He knew he sounded more like a hurt little boy than a man, but his family planned to leave him behind. The very idea hurt.

He was in the bedroom now, and they allowed him to sit down while his siblings dashed around, flinging clothing at him.

Rabbie pulled a blue-and-green Graham tartan kilt off his face to find his father standing in front of him.

"Isobel, please go help Catriona get ready." Da's tone meant no delay.

She threw a shirt to Fin and hurried out.

"Listen to me closely, Rabbie lad. We must be away from here with the Honours. Fin spotted a group of English soldiers just past the meadow. Ye ken two things verra well, and I'll nae be arguing with you aboot them. First, yer injured and sick and cannae travel in the snow without slowing us down. Second, ye must have feelings for Catriona ... ye kissed her. 'Tis best fer you both to be handfast before we leave you here alone."

The room spun and tilted. Rabbie was glad to be sitting down, even if Fin was on the floor shoving stockings on his feet as if he were a child.

"But, Da—"

His father's head shook, making his untidy mass of red hair move too. "I told ye, son. Nae arguments. "'Twill be done and soon. Catriona has agreed."

Then his face softened and he helped Rabbie into a clean, white linen shirt. "Ye are my first born, Rabbie. I will not see you perish for lack of shelter and rest. "Your Mamm would be glad to see this day of your marriage. Give it time. You and Catriona will be as happy as Moira and I were." A tear ran down Da's ruddy cheek and disappeared into his short beard.

Rabbie embraced his father for the first time in a long time. "I'll nae let you down,

Da. I'll be the man ye want me to be." His voice came out hoarse, so he cleared it. "We'll all be together again, I vow."

* * *

In less than an hour, Catriona was standing in her father's bedroom waiting to be called out to begin the handfasting ceremony. Isobel had helped her to dress in a full-sleeved white blouse under a dark-green velvet bodice with white laces up the front. A pretty, yellow underskirt that she had embroidered herself with navy-blue flowers peeked out of her dark-blue overskirt. Her best soft-soled slippers completed the outfit.

Isobel came over and handed her a sprig of shiny green holly leaves with red berries. "There are no flowers blooming with all this snow, but I thought these would work.

Catriona met her gaze and smiled. "Thank you … sister. Ye'll truly be my sister verra soon." Tears blurred her vision. How she wished her mother and little sister and her da could have been here today.

Isobel had to clear her throat before speaking. "I know my father is pushing this, but ye dinna have to marry Rabbie, if you dinna want him as your husband."

"I ken no one would force me, Isobel. But I do love Rabbie. He's all I can think of day and night. I dinna think I could stand being away from him. He's my friend and he's smart and handsome. I want him. I do."

"Come then, Cat, yer groom awaits."

As soon as Catriona stepped outside of the bedroom, Fin Graham was there to take her arm and escort her a few steps to where

117

Boyd and Rabbie waited in front of a cheerily blazing fireplace. Rabbie's falcon, Brisda, perched on a low crossbeam beside him. The bird was hooded to keep her calm, but she obviously knew that people were nearby by the cock of her head toward them.

The other Grahams were dressed for traveling, but Rabbie wore the same splendid plaid kilt and sash with white stockings and shirt he had worn the day he had first showed her the falcons. Even though his face was pale and one eye was nearly swollen shut and purple, Catriona thought Rabbie Graham was the most handsome man she'd ever seen in her life.

Fin dropped his hand and stepped away.

Rabbie's face lit up when he saw her and he grinned, a slash of white in a multi-colored bruised face.

"You're so beautiful, Cat," he whispered.

"Thank you." Catriona dropped her gaze to her shoes and then back up to his face. She grinned right back at him.

The Grand Falconer nodded at them both and began ...

"Do you, Robert Alexander Graham, take Catriona Dunn—"

"Marie."

Boyd paused. "... Catriona Marie Dunn to be your wife? To be her constant friend, her partner in life, and her true love?"

The words continued and, and after a moment's hesitation, they agreed when asked.

Then Boyd drew out a long, green ribbon from his pocket. "Please join hands."

He held their clasped hands—Catriona's left and Rabbie's right—and wrapped the ribbon tightly around them. He nodded to Rabbie.

"Ye are Blood of my Blood, and Bone of my Bone. I give you my Body that we Two might be one. I give ye my Spirit 'til our Life shall be Done."

With each word Rabbie spoke, he gazed searchingly at her face. She saw that he spoke the truth to her. She saw that he meant his words.

"Now you, Catriona." Boyd prompted her through the vow, helping her when her memory stumbled. But she spoke each word to Rabbie with her gaze locked on his clear blue eyes.

Then Boyd continued.

"Now you are bound, one to the other
With a tie not easy to break
Take the time of binding
Before the final vows are made
To learn what you need to know
To grow in wisdom and love
That your marriage will be strong
That your love will last
In this life and beyond."

Boyd stepped closer to Rabbie, unfastened the gold brooch on his sash, and lifted the sash off his shoulder before handing it back to him.

Rabbie took the sash and with his one free hand, draped it over Catriona's shoulder. Isobel took the brooch and pinned the ends of the sash at Catriona's waist.

"I've no ring fer ye, Catriona. This sash will mark you as a Graham now, as my wife, Catriona Graham.

"Thank ye, husband. I've something for you." She glanced at Isobel, who turned and picked up a basket from the floor beside her. She held it for Catriona so she could lift the cloth and draw out a loaf of bread.

"This is not as fine as a clan sash, but 'tis a symbol of how our love will nourish us both body and soul … together."

Rabbie accepted the loaf and held it while she pulled off a piece and fed it to him. He did the same for her.

"Welcome to the family, daughter!"

Catriona and Rabbie were engulfed in hugs from the rest of the Grahams. They were freed from the ribbon, and the handfasting ceremony came to an end.

* * *

Twilight crept in, casting gloomy shadows over everything when the Graham family donned their packs and stepped outside of the cottage.

Boyd carried the golden crown, with its gemstones and pearls, wrapped in cloth and hidden in his pack. Isobel now carried the silver gilt sceptre. Catriona had been enthralled with the images of the dolphins, the Virgin Mary, and baby Christ that appeared on the head of the sceptre rod.

Fin carried the sword and scabbard in his pack. Unfortunately, they had been forced to break the sword in two to conceal the long blade and silver gilt handle.

The old and very valuable regalia were symbols of Scotland and symbols of their land and heritage. Rabbie knew his family had been honoured to be chosen to ensure the safety of the Scottish Crown Jewels housed in their packs.

Along with the supplies and regalia, they took Fin's falcon, Grizel, and the other two peregrines to release them to the sky. With luck, they could call them back to their fists later. Brisda belonged to Rabbie, so she stayed behind in the cottage.

Rabbie stood leaning against the door jam, watching the birds soar high up into the darkening sky. Catriona stood beside him. She was his wife now, and he would love and protect her always. But he still mentally cursed the lingering weakness of his body as he bid goodbye to his family.

Da was right to leave him behind; he would only slow them down. On the other hand, his disability had led the way to his marriage to Catriona, which was a blessing to be sure. He watched until he could no longer see the others as they disappeared into the trees and gathering gloom.

"We will see them again. If they've not returned by spring, we can go after them, Rabbie."

Bless her. How he loved Catriona, she knew just what to say to encourage him. But her words drove home the truth of it. They would be trapped here, in this small baker's cottage for months to come. His shoulders drooped and his back throbbed. He felt ill. Perhaps the fever was returning.

Catriona took his hand, pulled him inside, then shut and barred the door against the wind. Somewhere outside, a lone wolf howled.

She led him past the table with the soiled dishes and remains of their modest wedding feast. They walked to Cináed's bedroom … their bedroom now, with its large wood-framed bed and thick, stuffed mattress.

"Come, Rabbie." Catriona's voice was low and sultry, "'Tis our wedding night. Shall we not enjoy it?"

The realization hit his brain and body at the same time. It *is* our wedding night, mine, and the woman I love. "I verra much want to enjoy it with you, *mo leannan*.

Sitting beside Catriona on the bed, Rabbie wrestled off his kilt and stockings while his bride's soft hands explored every inch of his exposed skin. He moaned. His anatomy responded vigorously and she noticed.

"Rabbie, I've never seen a naked man before. Are ye perhaps bigger than most?"

Although he liked to think that he might be extra manly, he needed to tell her the truth. A marriage had to be based on truth.

"Nay, I am but average."

"But … I am nay so large as that." Her expression showed her doubt, and he realized anew how innocent and untouched she was.

"Dinna fash yerself, Cat, you will be just fine."

Standing naked in front of her, he helped her take off her wedding clothing. She didn't take her eyes off his body. When she wrapped her slender fingers around his shaft, he nearly swallowed his tongue.

Rabbie sucked in a breath and tried to speak. Nothing came out. He started again and put a hand on top of hers to stop her movements so he could force out a few words.

"No rush, *mo leannan*.

He bent toward her, leaning in to take her lips and cradling the back of her head with one hand as she lay back on the blankets.

The kiss grew to be long, deep, and sensual. Their tongues danced. He detected the faint taste of her flaky pastries lingering in her silky mouth. Catriona was truly a sweet treat to be savored slowly and thoroughly, and Rabbie fully intended to do this.

Breaking the kiss, he balanced on his knees, straddling her hips. By the moonlight filtering through the window, Rabbie's hungry gaze swept over every luscious hill and valley she possessed.

She gave him a shy smile then lifted both hands to caress his shoulders and chest.

He couldn't suppress a groan when her hands slid down his sides to his thighs. Dipping his head, he nibbled down her neck until he licked one rosy nibble.

Catriona moaned, so Rabbie intensified his attention to first one breast then the other.

"Please," she whispered, and he knew what she wanted.

A split second later she guided him inside and only physicality existed.

His world shrank to her and only her. The slide of sleek, damp skin against skin. The taste of her lips, her breasts, her womanhood. The sweet scent of her silky chestnut hair. The sight of her wide, passionate gaze meeting his. The sound of breathless pants and whispered pleasure. All of these and more coalesced into a crescendo of exquisite sexual release, and it left them both tangled in each other's arms and speechless.

Chapter 14

Brisda's soft, "skree", woke Rabbie, galvanizing him into action almost before he realized what he was doing. Standing barefoot on the packed-dirt floor, he heard rustling noises coming from the other room.

"Get up and get dressed, Cat. Someone's in the main room," he whispered as he pulled on breeches and a shirt. "Dress warmly, take Brisda, and go out through the window. I'll take care of those bastards. Let the falcon loose and hide!"

Lucky for him, his beloved new wife trusted his judgment and quickly followed his urgent requests. Knife in hand, Rabbie eased open the bedroom door a crack.

The fireplace in the center of the main room still held embers glowing with enough light for him to see two figures creeping through the room. One man pulled loaves of bread and dried meats out of their baskets, scattering the food everywhere. The other yanked blankets and clothing out of the freestanding wardrobe. They were obviously looking for something. Based on their military uniforms, Rabbie assumed they were on a mission to find the Honours of Scotland. Thankfully, his family had left with the valuable regalia over two weeks ago.

Rabbie yanked open the door and stepped through. He held the knife where they could see it and advanced slowly.

DIANE WYLIE

"Stop right now and leave, and I'll allow you to live."

A derisive chuckle from the man at the wardrobe gave Rabbie his answer. "Look, Haversham, he's got a puny knife. Show him what you've got.

Haversham had a flintlock pistol, which he waved around carelessly. "I thinks me gun wins over your knife, mate." Then he leveled the gun at Rabbie's midsection and pulled back the hammer with a decisive click. "Where's them crown j—"

Thunk.

Haversham's mouth dropped open, and the gun thumped to the floor as the man crumpled with a knife protruding from his chest.

His unarmed companion wasted no time. He heaved an armful of clothing at the fireplace. The cloth caught quickly with an ominous whoosh. In seconds, flames spread across one of Catriona's skirts, down the tangle of cloth to the dropped pile, and up the wooden wardrobe.

Rabbie pulled his second knife from his waistband and threw it at the fleeing soldier. It landed between the man's shoulder blades, and he was dead before he hit the floor.

Coughing and cursing, Rabbie tried to beat out the flames with one of his deceased father-in-law's large shirts. *I canna let Catriona's home burn!*

Hungry yellow flames leaped up the tall wardrobe and raced up to the thatched roof. Rabbie knew this little stone cottage could be destroyed in minutes. Still, he tried once more and scrambled to throw a bucket of washing water onto the flames.

It was no use.

"No!" Her scream tore through him as she ran in behind him. "Ye canna let it burn!" Pulling up a braided rug, Catriona beat on the growing flames.

"It's no use, Cat!"

But she paid no heed to his words.

Rabbie ran to the bedroom to get his extra knives, boots, coat, some clothes for his wife, and a few other things they would need.

Catriona coughed in the mounting smoke, but continued to throw the rug on the spreading fire. She didn't realize or didn't care that the rug itself was burning.

"Catriona! Come!"

"No! No! No!"

Shifting everything to one arm, Rabbie raced over to her and grabbed his wife by the waist. He hauled her outside, even as she kicked and fought him while screaming in his ear.

"Let me go, Rabbie! I can save it!"

After carrying her away from the cottage, he laid her down in the snow and pinned her there with his body. He looked back over his shoulder.

Orange and yellow flames engulfed the entire roof now and licked the front door frame as smoke poured out of the open doorway.

Catriona fought like a wildcat, hitting him with her fists, and even biting him on the shoulder.

"Cat! Cat! Look for yourself! No one can save the cottage."

Finally, she turned her head to see. Her head dropped and her body went limp under him. Reality had sunk in.

He rolled to a sitting position and pulled her into his lap. Vibrations ran through her body and her shoulders shuddered as she began to sob.

"Hush, *mo leannan*, 'twill be all right. You'll see." Rabbie stroked her silky hair. "We'll have a better house before ye ken it."

"No!" To his shock, she shoved him backward and jumped up. "Before I met ye, Rabbie Graham, my life may have been boring, but I had my Da, and we were happy in our cottage … the one he built for my mother."

Rabbie lay in the snow on his itchy, healing back and watched his new wife pace back and forth, silhouetted by the orange glow of the fire behind her. Her long, black hair seemed to have a life of its own as it fluttered and flew about.

"There will never be a 'better house,' Rabbie, because that," she flung an arm toward the burning cottage, "was the best house on the face of this earth. Do you ken why it was the best? Do ye?"

He gave no answer.

"Because it was made with love. Love! Do ye ken what that is, because I dinna think you do."

Rabbie decided a good course of action here would be to let Catriona say what she would. He had a sister and learned how a response was not always needed or wanted.

"Love isna something ye decide to have because you want to 'do the right thing' and obey yer Da's wishes. Isobel told me that you loved me, but you never did, Rabbie."

Had he never said the words? Were they not part of the handfasting ceremony? He wasn't sure. It had gone by so quickly, and he'd been ill at the time.

The hem of Catriona's night rail under her coat dragged in the snow as she paced. "Aye, we've had intercourse like a married couple that loves each other, but is that all there is to a marriage? Before my mamm died, I knew she and Da loved each other. His face said so, the little touches on her arm said so, and the way they acted together said so."

She stopped in front of Rabbie, who had propped himself up on his elbows to watch her.

"You don't give me what I need, Rabbie."

Her voice was so low and sad. He wanted to give her what she needed, but he didn't know what it was. They'd been married for two weeks and he'd sensed her dissatisfaction growing. She seemed satiated after their lovemaking, so he didn't think that was the problem. *Be brave and ask her.*

He stood and took her by the shoulders. She didn't resist. "What do you need, Cat? I would pull down the moon for you, if ye but asked. I am but an unobservant man, unschooled in the way of marriage."

"I dinna need the moon, Rabbie. I need you … all of you. I need your affection; yer thoughts and dreams. I need you to be what ye vowed … my constant friend, my partner, and my true love."

Her words hurt. He thought he'd been acting as a true husband should. How had he failed her?

He dropped his hands. "Do you wish we'd never wed, Catriona? Do ye want us to be apart?"

"Nay, Rabbie."

But she didn't touch him. She turned her back on him to gaze at the now-dying fire.

"I suppose ye dinna really deserve the blame for this, but I need peace in my life. I canna abide the trouble and turmoil as has come with knowing ye."

He couldn't keep away from her and came up behind her to wrap his arms around her slim body and lay his cheek against her soft hair.

"I swear that none of this was my doing, Cat. And I swear before God and all that is holy that I do love ye. I've loved you since those beautiful eyes of yours looked up at me from the ground the day I met you in the forest and slayed that boar." He drew in a deep breath before continuing.

'Twas the right thing to do, to be handfast before we were alone, that is true. But I did it happily. No one, not even the Grand Falconer himself could have forced me to marry you had I not wanted it."

* * *

Rabbie said all the right words, but Catriona didn't feel any better. She would worry about that later. Right now, they needed shelter for the night.

She sighed and turned in his arms to face him. "Yer words are verra nice, but they canna bring back my home or my Da."

"Oh, Cat, it is so sorry I am that I canna do that for ye. I would, if I could." He reached up and wiped the cold tears from her cheeks with his thumbs, and her anger decreased a wee bit.

She took one of his hands, pulled it away from her face, and began to lead him toward the only building left, the freestanding bakehouse with its baking ovens. "Come, we'll sleep in the bakehouse and talk in the morning."

Then she stopped and tilted her head to the sky. "Will you call Brisda back?"

"Nay, I'll call her back in the morning. She'll be fine."

Cat nodded, dropped his hand, and left him to gather what was left of their belongings while she walked through the snow to the small stone building.

With any luck, no more English soldiers would come seeking the Honours of Scotland this night.

Once inside the bakehouse, Catriona felt her throat tighten once more as she went about lighting a few candles. How many hours had she and Da worked side by side to make their breads, rolls, and pastries? Too many to count. She could see him in her mind's eye, black beard and hair coated with flour, whistling a tune as he worked the dough.

131

Rabbie walked in behind her, dropped his burdens on a table and once again wrapped his arms around her. "Memories?"

"Aye." Her voice cracked as she answered.

This was the first time her husband had come into the bakehouse. During his recovery, he'd kept to the cottage while she came out here to do a small amount of baking for the two of them. The same bags of flour still lay in rows on the shelves. The same precious mixing bowls still sat ready for use on the wooden table. Why did the place seem so empty and sorrowful now? Why had the loss hit her anew tonight?

"Come, *mo leannan*. I have blankets. Shall we try to get comfortable on the big table? 'Twill be warmer than the floor." Rabbie moved the bowls and implements off the table, spread one blanket down, and then offered her a hand up. So she got on top of the table and lay down. He climbed up beside her, pulled her close, and then cocooned them under a second blanket.

Rabbie did make her feel safe, but the hole in her heart remained wide open and painful.

She loved Rabbie. Of course she did. From the moment she first saw him riding into Dunnottar on his horse, with his falcon by his side, she had fallen for this man hard. But if death and destruction were part of being his wife, could she bear it?

Chapter 15

After a fitful sleep, Catriona emerged from the bakehouse and walked the short distance to the blackened ruins of the only home she'd known.

All of her tears were gone, and her eyes were gritty and dry. An awful, smoky smell spread out from the pile of stones and burned-out timbers.

Searching around for a bit, she found a nice-sized stick and began to poke around in the ruins for anything salvageable. Although the snow had stopped, it had melted on the remains and created a black, soggy mess.

There! One of my boots! She had run outside last night in her shoes. *Where is the other one?* Da had saved for months to get the sturdy leather boots for her birthday last year. Finding them was important.

Black water dripped off the boot as she lifted it out of the rubble, turned it upside down, and drained it.

"I found your other bootie, Cat!"

Rabbie's triumphant yell had her swinging in his direction. Feet planted wide over a fallen timber, he also held the boot in his hand upside down to drain it.

"'Tis a little scorched on the top, but I think you can wear it."

The heart-stopping grin on his tired face struck Catriona like a blow. Rabbie truly did try his best to please her. Could it be that she took out her unhappiness on him needlessly?

She came to him, accepted the second boot, and gave him a quick kiss on his whiskered cheek.

"Thank ye, husband."

Crinkles appeared in the corners of his blue eyes as another smile curved upward. "Dinna fash yerself, we'll find what we can here, get a bite to eat, and talk about what to do."

Then he leaned forward, took her by the shoulders and pressed his warm, sensual lips to hers. By the time he broke off that kiss, Catriona's body tingled from head to toe. She was left panting for breath and highly aroused.

Heehaw. Heehaw. Heehaw.

They both swiveled to the noise.

A gray, shaggy donkey with black on the tips of its long ears stood there, watching them with big brown eyes. It stuck out its head and brayed again.

"Roger!"

Catriona ran to the creature, dropped her boots, and threw her arms around its neck. "Look, Rabbie, 'tis Roger come home!" She rubbed her cheek against the donkey's furry head, which only came to her shoulders. Her little friend had come back.

"Where has the animal been all this time?" Rabbie came over and inspected Roger for signs of injury. He even lifted each of the donkey's legs to inspect his hooves.

"Is he okay?"

Rabbie straightened, brushed off his hands, and faced her. "He seems to have nay problems other than hungry ..."

Roger's teeth caught hold of Catriona's coat. Just then, Rabbie's stomach growled and he chuckled.

"... Like me."

"This day is improving, laddie." Catriona glanced at Rabbie then took hold of Roger's bridle and led the donkey toward the bakehouse. "I believe we have some bread and honey for you, Rabbie, and some horsebread for our mighty stead."

* * *

Rabbie picked up Catriona's wet boots and followed behind his wife and her donkey. From his view, Catriona's skirts swung back and forth, as she walked. The urge to put his hands on those hips to feel their sway hit him, but he restrained himself. Her mood had improved and he wasn't going to ruin it with a gesture she might not appreciate right now. Perhaps she would allow him some liberties later. As his health had improved over the past two weeks, his appetite for his wife's attentions had increased tremendously. He didn't think he would ever get enough of her.

Although he really wanted to take Catriona on the table now and ravish her with kisses from head to toe, he settled for food. There were two chairs in the bakehouse, so they sat across from each other to eat the bread that Catriona had baked early in the morning. The delicious smell of bread mingled with the smoky burned-cottage smell.

Catriona placed her boots in the still-warm oven to dry.

"What will we do now? Just live in the bakehouse?" Catriona's dark brows drew together with worry.

"Would you like to see if we can go back to Dunnottar and live in the castle? I'm not sure if the English have taken it or not. If our men-at-arms prevailed, we should be able to live in my house."

Conflicting emotions flitted across her pretty face—excitement, doubt, sorrow, and then anxiety.

"Will I still be able to bake?"

"Och, aye. Mamm had bakehouse privileges, and as my wife, ye will too."

She glanced around her at the tiny bakehouse. "It pains me to leave this place, but 'twould be foolish to stay here with the British hunting for the Honours."

His mouth tugged up at the corners, and he stood, holding a hand out to her. "Come let us see what else we can find of yours, call Brisda back, pack up Roger, and go back to Dunnottar.

But Catriona didn't move, she just held his gaze with troubled green eyes. "What about your family? Do ye not want to follow them?"

"They are verra smart people, probably more so than me. I've nae worries on their account. I'm sure they'll find a safe place for the regalia and come home to Dunnottar Castle again." He leaned over and took her elbow to urge her to her feet. "All will be well."

* * *

After the attack by the English soldiers, Rabbie had decided they should travel at night. He told her their progress would be slower but safer.

"How do ye ken we're going the right way?" Catriona had one hand on Roger's withers to guide her while Rabbie led the animal, which carried their meager belongings on its back.

"Have you nay faith in your husband, lass? Brisda and I have hunted these woods for years." The good humor in his voice carried back to where she walked, though he was just a moving figure in the darkness.

"Och, I forgot about your falcon. Where is she?"

"She's following. You canna hear or see her, but she is with us, riding the air currents above."

"Do ye think she kens she is going home?" Catriona kept her voice low. They were crossing open ground now, and she knew how well the Scottish winds could carry sound out here.

"Perhaps. Watch for a large boulder ahead. Dinna walk into it."

He warned her just in time. She had to squeeze up against Roger's furry side to avoid the huge rock.

"'Tis a good landmark for our journey home."

Catriona had to take his word on this. Having only traveled a few times to Dunnottar, she could not have found her way back to the castle alone.

A cold wind tried to pull the hood off her head, and she grabbed it with her free hand. The ground under her rescued boots was rocky and frozen. Thick clouds filled the sky when she glanced up to locate Rabbie's falcon. A large-winged bird soared high in the sky, silhouetted against a moonlit break in the clouds. Brisda was up there. The thought was oddly comforting.

The three of them walked on and on.

After what seemed like a long time, Rabbie slowed the donkey to a stop then walked back to her.

"Time for you and Roger to hide while I go to the gatehouse. I need to see who stands guard … friend or foe."

"Will you stay safe in the shadows then, Rabbie?"

"Aye, will you wait, quiet as a mouse for me until I come get ye?"

"Och, aye, husband. I understand."

Taking hold of Roger's bridle, Rabbie led the animal and Catriona to a small copse of scrubby bushes. He handed her the lead.

"Get as comfortable as you can. Maybe sleep a bit. This may take some time, but I'll come back for ye."

Then he drew her into a fierce hug and squeezed the air out of her. She let out an involuntary squeak of surprise that was quickly muffled by his mouth descending on hers. As was his wont lately, he proceeded to kiss her breathless and tingly. Then abruptly, he released her. She staggered back a bit so he steadied her with a hand on her arm.

"Stay hidden, *mo leannan.*"

"I will," was all she managed to say before he turned and disappeared into the night.

* * *

Isobel used to tease him, saying he could see in the dark like a cat. Well, his good eyesight came in very handy tonight as he walked up the steep, exposed road toward the gatehouse. Every few seconds, he stopped stock-still to look in every direction and to listen hard for any signs that someone was about.

Silence filled his ears, save the ever-present Highland wind coming off the North Sea.

Rabbie moved on. He came to the gatehouse. Across the road, Benholm's Lodge stood silent and dark. A lack of windows on this side of Benholm's reassured Rabbie that he had thus far escaped detection.

No guards stood in their normal stations outside the gatehouse. Their absence seemed highly unusual. If the English had prevailed, they would have posted guards, and if the Scots had defeated them, Shamas or Ian should be keeping watch.

Rabbie's heart beat faster and his hands began to sweat.

What will I find inside Dunnottar?

He drew his dirk from the sheath at his waist, grateful for the feel of a weapon in his hand.

Crouching low, Rabbie slipped past the gatehouse. The heavy metal portcullis was raised, allowing him free access to the tunnel beyond it. He knew that once he went inside the tunnel, he could easily be trapped.

Switching the dirk to his left hand, he wiped the right palm on his breeches and took the knife in his dominant hand once more. He sucked in a deep breath and stepped inside the damp darkness, feeling along the rough tunnel wall as he went.

The recognizable stench of something dead or rotten reached his nostrils and he nearly gagged.

Something wasn't right. The Dunnottar inhabitants would never allow an animal to die in the tunnel without clearing it away. The tunnels were used too frequently to allow this to happen.

Still keeping one hand on the wall, Rabbie picked up his pace. He had to find out what had happened inside and get back to Catriona.

"Oof!"

He tripped and fell, landing on something big, soft, and nauseating. His dirk clattered onto stones somewhere in the dark as he immediately rolled away.

He had fallen on the source of the stench! A dead body!

Down on hands and knees, he frantically felt around, blindly searching for his dagger.

"Ow." He found it.

After locating the handle, he picked up his weapon, stuck the bleeding finger in his mouth, and relocated the tunnel wall. Now was no time to delay.

Swallowing hard, he held onto the stones and stepped backward gingerly until he found the soft pile of remains. Knowing the direction he had fallen, he figured out which way he needed to go to enter the castle, stepped into the middle of the tunnel, and began to trot toward the end that led to the courtyard.

Is anyone left alive in Dunnottar castle?

Chapter 16

Catriona molded the dough into yet another loaf. Da took a flat piece of metal out of the oven and slid six more hot loaves onto the table to join the several dozen already crowding the wooden surface from end to end.

"This is far more than we can sell, Da. So much will go to waste," she protested.

"Cat. Cat." The soft voice woke her from her dreams, and she lifted her head from Roger the donkey's side as he lay with his legs tucked under him. The animal had not moved in response to her husband's appearance. Roger had accepted Rabbie.

"Rabbie! Is everything all right?"

He dropped down beside her and got under the blankets. His clothes smelled of fresh air and smoke.

"The castle's abandoned. Everyone seems to be dead or gone. I couldna find a living soul. The Graham house, like yours, has been burned. Now mind, I didna investigate every room. In the morning, we'll both go inside to see if we can find any survivors and some food. I dinna think the English soldiers are there. No guards stood outside."

"Oh, no, Rabbie! They are all gone?"

"We will find out tomorrow. Come, *mo leannan*, lay down your head and let us sleep. Roger will give us fair warning of any intruders."

As if he were in their bed, Rabbie urged her to face away from him, gathered her

142

against his chest, and with one arm securely wrapped around her middle, he soon relaxed. From his even breathing, she knew he slept, and she was finally able to settle down too.

Roger turned to gaze at them, then faced forward again and shut his brown eyes. His big donkey ears remained on high alert as they swiveled to catch any noise.

Catriona tried to relax and stop worrying about what they would find by light of day, but it took some time before she could accomplish this and join her companions in slumber.

A light gray sky met her gaze when she awoke to the sensation of soft lips on her exposed neck.

"Would you care to let me taste your wares this morn, my sweet baker?" Rabbie's whisper tickled her ear.

She gave the teasing request careful consideration for a moment before answering. "Aye, but only if ye promise to be a regular customer."

The rumble in his chest as he chuckled sent a rush of liquid heat throughout her body.

In a thrice, he had rolled them both away from the donkey and was unfastening her bodice.

"Och, I promise. I've a verra healthy appetite."

He took one of her nipples in his mouth, drawing it in and out between his teeth, eliciting a strong thrill of anticipation throughout Catriona's body.

"Mmmm, you are delicious, my lass."

"You like what I have to offer, my husband?"

"Aye, verra much." He drew out the middle word, deepening his Scots accent.

"Let me see what you have to offer now." With that, she put her hand inside his breeches to find his warm member. He groaned. He was ready.

* * *

Before they stepped into the Dunnottar tunnels this time, Rabbie stopped and used a flint to ignite the torch he had made from dried grass tied to a hefty stick.

The flame lasted all the way through the first tunnel, allowing them to avoid not just one but three dead bodies inside.

They were halfway into the second tunnel when the flame burned out. He dropped the torch and held onto Catriona's hand as he led the donkey. Although the day had dawned heavy with snow clouds, a small circle of light still showed them the end of the tunnel.

Rabbie's respect for his wife grew with each passing moment. This was no hysterical woman. She did stay close to his side, but she held her head high and spoke very little as they traveled, despite the horrors of dead men with arrows protruding from their chests. Her face was very pale, and her eyes were wide when they finally emerged into the castle courtyard.

The devastation took Rabbie aback too, even though he had an inkling of it when he investigated the night before.

It appeared that every wooden structure inside the castle walls had been burned to some degree. Even the market tables were scorched or demolished to splinters of wood. A pristine coating of snow blanketed everything, adding to the feeling of death and finality.

Even worse than the destruction, was the loss of life. Bodies were left where they were killed. Most appeared to be Dunnottar's men-at-arms, but some were dressed as peasants and others wore the red coats of the English.

Rabbie exchanged glances with Catriona, but neither spoke. Slowly, he led the way toward what was left of the mews, where the Graham falcons had been housed.

Multiple fresh graves had been dug in the small castle cemetery where Da said they had buried his mother and Cináed Dunn. Not everyone had perished in the initial attack since some of the dead had been buried. It had taken some time to defeat Dunnottar.

"We'll visit our parents later, Cat."

She just nodded.

Her exhaustion was written in dark circles under her beautiful eyes, the slump of her shoulders, and the drag in her step. Her hair had partially escaped from the braid going down her back, and the bottoms of her coat and skirt were liberally covered with dirt.

Rabbie longed to give her a luxurious tub of hot water. He wanted to join her in it and soap up her exquisite body. The daydream was incongruous with their surroundings, so he reluctantly let it go. As soon as he could, though, he would pamper her terribly.

A falcon suddenly dropped out of the sky, flying so close that Rabbie felt the rush of air against his cheek from her wings.

"Look, Rabbie! Brisda!" Catriona's voice rang with pleasure.

The peregrine falcon flew past them twice before she landed on a hitching post that still stood in front of Rabbie's ruined childhood home. Her bright bird eyes fixed on him and she cocked her head. In her talons, she held a dead rat.

"She found us, Cat. I knew she would." He tried to put some life and optimism into his voice while he tied the donkey to the same post.

Brisda watched Rabbie approach and allowed him to stroke her head before she bent to eat her meal.

All cheerfulness fled as he stepped into the remains of the mews. Thankfully, he couldn't see the bodies of any falcons inside the tangle of fallen timbers.

Catriona bent and plucked a small piece of leather out of the rubble. She handed it to Rabbie. "It looks like one of the hoods survived."

"Aye. 'Twill come in useful later. I can get more fledglings from the nest and train new birds."

The first real smile he's seen in some time spread across Catriona's face. "Aye, Rabbie, you can become a Grand Falconer too."

"I'd like that, my love, but first we need food, clothing, and supplies. Shall we look and see what we can use? We'll start here with falconry items."

Rabbie found an empty sack that had escaped the flames. They filled it with two pairs of jesses, complete with bells; three water bowls; another hood; and a small cage for capturing fledglings.

"Rabbie, you dinna need to look about inside your ruined house, if it bothers you. I can do it alone. I'll bring out what we can use."

Somehow, Catriona had sensed his reluctance to go inside the burned out shell that was his house. Knowing that Mamm was gone, and the scene of his childhood memories was destroyed, made going inside unbearable.

His throat constricted and his vision blurred. Now he knew what Cat had gone through after her childhood cottage was burned.

Rabbie went to his wife and wrapped his arms around her. "Thank ye, *mo leannan*. You are my heart and soul."

She laid her head against his chest, just under his chin on his heart. "No need for thanks. We need to help each other. Remember, 'Blood of my Blood' …"

"… and, 'Bone of my Bone'," he finished the line from their handfasting ceremony.

"We two are one, Rabbie."

"Aye, we are."

Releasing her, he stepped back, rubbed both hands over his face, and sucked in a deep breath. "While ye look for anything we can use, I'll go see if there are any living people here in Dunnottar. It may take me some time to cover the whole place. I'll bring back anything useful or edible … or living."

Catriona glanced at the burned out building then back at him. "Take Roger with ye, in case you need him. Maybe you can find a cart?"

"Good thinking. I ken I married a smart woman."

Rabbie walked over to the donkey and untied his reins from the post.

"Rabbie?"

"Aye?" He swiveled toward Catriona.

"What will we do now that we have no home?" Her voice wobbled a bit, but she got the words out.

He gave her a smile. "Ye are my home, Catriona. As long as we're together, I am home."

Tears ran down her face, leaving wet tracks on her smudged cheeks.

Rabbie opened his arms and she rushed back into his embrace. "Dinnae cry, Cat." Her hair was soft under his caress. "How would you feel about setting out to find the rest of my family? We cannae stay here alone. We'd starve."

She nodded against his chest. "Aye, seems the best thing."

"Right then, let us be about our tasks while the day is young."

Catriona dropped her arms and stepped back, swiping the moisture from her eyes and sniffing.

Rabbie bent to retrieve his *sgain dubh* from his stocking and, holding it by the blade, handed it to her. "I'd feel better if ye had protection."

Her eyes widened at first, but then an expression of grim determination settled on her face, and she accepted the knife. "My Da taught me how to handle this type of weapon. I never thought I'd really need to use what he taught me."

"I'll be hoping ye dinna have to use that knife." Rabbie gave her a quick kiss on the cheek. Any more physical contact than that, and he'd be laying her down anywhere he could.

* * *

She watched him walk away leading their little donkey. His long, purposeful stride reminded her that their daylight hours were limited.

Turning back toward the remains of the building, her gaze landed on Rabbie's falcon. The bird swallowed the last bit of rat meat, stared at Catriona for a second, and then spread her wings to follow her master.

The whole idea of teaching wild falcons to do your bidding seemed amazing to Catriona. She could not always get her donkey to move when and where she wanted, and her family had owned him for at least ten years.

Heaving a sigh, Catriona stepped over the threshold into the remnants of the Grahams' home. The thatched roof was gone, which actually helped her to see what was left. Spying an iron fireplace poker, she retrieved it and began to poke around in the blackened, snow-soggy, smelly mess.

Because she had spent some time inside this house, she remembered its layout. The main room lay just within the front door. At the opposite end from the door, the large stone fireplace still stood with a big iron cauldron suspended inside. Although the cauldron would be nice to have in a new home, she rejected it as too heavy for travel.

The fire had to have been intense, and she wondered what had set it off. When the English stormed the castle, did they use flaming arrows? She had once heard a couple of young boys talking about setting fire to arrows and shooting them.

Nothing was any good in the main room. She moved to the remains of the small room that Rabbie and his brother Fin shared. Moving aside snow and underlying burnt straw, Catriona found a mostly undamaged wooden toy horse. She could imagine Rabbie as a little boy with his dark curls and big blue eyes. He was probably adorable.

Rabbie had changed since the early days when they had first met. They'd only known each other for a relatively short time, but so much had happened. He'd seemed to be a lad in the beginning, strutting around in his fine kilt and plaid, and showing her the falcons. Now, his whole demeanor had grown more serious and mature. Now, Rabbie Graham was a man in his words and actions.

Had the beating changed him, or was it the loss of his mother, or maybe both?

Had she changed too? She certainly felt older. She had to look to her own survival now that her Da was gone. Actually, she and her husband needed to work together for their very survival. Life had not seemed easy before all of this, but looking back, she realized it had been very simple by comparison.

Catriona tucked the wooden horse into her coat pocket. Rabbie might like it.

After hours of poking and searching, she found a decent pair of breeches, two pots, one clay drinking vessel, a smoky undamaged blanket, a tarnished silver hand mirror, some dried strips of meat, a sack of flour, and an old oil lamp.

She went into the remains of Isobel's bedroom and found a metal heart-shaped locket on a chain. It joined the toy horse in her coat pocket.

As she mused on the idea of a suitor giving the locket to Isobel, Rabbie's falcon arrived on a silent disturbance of air. It landed on a scarred and charred wooden table nearby.

"Greetings, Brisda." Catriona craned her neck to look over the rubble to the courtyard outside. "Is Rabbie coming?"

In the distance, she could see Rabbie coming toward her. He led Roger, who appeared to be pulling a small wooden cart.

Her heart leaped and beat faster as soon as she saw her husband. He stirred her senses tremendously.

Brushing off her hands, she climbed over a fallen board and a pile of rubble to get out of the house.

As he approached, the cart came into view. It appeared to be full of things. She hoped he'd had better luck finding food than she had.

But no one else came along with Rabbie. That realization made her heart sink. Was there no one left alive here in Dunnottar castle?

Leaving the house behind, she walked toward Rabbie.

"I have good news, Catriona. It seems that most of the people of Dunnottar were not killed by the English. They were ordered to leave."

A snuffling noise came from the cart, and Catriona glanced in its direction. "Did ye find an animal?"

"No—"

The pile of clothing and goods moved, and a little boy's dark head popped up. His face was dirty and streaked with tears. "I want my mamm," he cried.

She whirled around to face Rabbie. "Who is this lad, and who is his mother?"

Rabbie walked to the wagon and lifted the young boy into his arms, wiping away the boy's tears with his shirtsleeve.

"Catriona, this is young William Ogilvie, son of the governor and his wife. William, this is my wife, Catriona Graham, you can call her Cat, if ye like."

After forcing the shock off her face, Catriona came closer and patted the boy's back. The lad buried his face in Rabbie's neck and refused to look at her.

"I'm happy to meet ye, Willam." She met Rabbie's gaze. "Do you ken where his mamm might be?"

"William says his nurse told him to hide when the bad men came, so he did. Poor wee lad came out of the cabinet to find himself alone. Everyone had either left or died in battle. 'Tis a horrible thing for a lad of five summers to be left to fend for himself. I told him we would be his Da and Mamm until we can find them.

"Och, poor thing. We will do as Rabbie says, William. We'll take care of you until we find them." She gave William's back another pat and turned back to the cart. "Did ye find food, Rabbie?"

"Aye, William here is a smart laddie. He went straight to the food pantry and stayed there. I had a wee bit o' trouble coaxing him out, but he kens we are not the English devils."

Catriona lifted aside a blanket to reveal several barrels containing smoked fish, flour, pickled eggs, salted pork, and whiskey. There was also a wheel of cheese and a small barrel of butter.

"Wonderful! We've food to last us a while."

Rabbie beamed, put William on his feet, and reached into the cart. "Look what I got for ye, Cat."

Between his hands, dangling like the sign handing in front of a seedy pub, was a large, wrinkled corset with whalebone ribs and dark sweat stains under the armpit areas.

"Rabbie Graham! Do ye think me fat?" Catriona snatched the offending garment from his hands while little William laughed.

"N-no … I-I just thought, since ye didna have one, ye might like it."

"Ye thought wrong." Catriona threw the corset with all her might toward a pile of burned objects. "I dinna want one … ever!"

She went to their newfound little boy and took his hand. "Come, William, can ye show me where we can find ye some clothes? We are all taking a long trip and will need some warm clothing for you. We'll find your family and Rabbie's as well.

They headed back to the abandoned palace of Dunnottar Castle together. Rabbie came up to take William's other hand, still leading the donkey and cart.

Brisda swooped down low in front of them, then lifted up and circled back to fly above her master. Catriona knew the falcon would stay with them as they searched together for their missing family. The journey would be hazardous, but love of family would keep them strong … and Catriona was a Graham clan member now. She glanced at her husband. No matter what the future held, they were bound together as one, and nothing, not even the loss of their homes, would kept the Scottish down.

The Scottish Falconers by Diane Wylie

Follow the Graham family falconers as they continue their mission to protect the sacred Scottish regalia and preserve this valuable piece of history.

Book One: Besieged
Book Two: Hunted
Book Three: Displaced

The Scottish Falconers
Book Two: Hunted
Chapter 1
Preview

March 1652
Scotland

Panting heavily, Isobel Graham ran through the brambles and brush, splashed through a small stream, and scaled the muddy bank before reaching the spot where her peregrine falcon, Latharna had brought down a large duck. The falcon had already begun to pluck out the dull brown feathers of its prey.

Isobel stopped a few feet away and whistled sharply. Latharna raised her head and regarded Isobel with her black eyes for a heartbeat or two. Then she spread her large gray and brown wings to lift, soar a short distance, and land on Isobel's gloved hand. She immediately ate the skinned rat her mistress held as Isobel caught the leather jesses on the birds legs between her fingers to keep the falcon with her.

"Och, Latharna, I didna think ye'd come to me. That's a good girl." Isobel sucked in another breath. "I'm wishing we had a bonnie retriever dog to chase down the kill."

Isobel had lost her falcon during the siege at Dunnottar Castle a month ago, but the bird had found the Graham family again as they headed north, away from the carnage.

Still carrying the falcon, Isobel stepped over and picked up the dead duck by its feet.

"My brother Rabbie would be happy to ken ye found us, just like his Brisda found him. He helped me train ye, do you remember?" Isobel stroked the falcon's breast with one finger before placing the finely tooled leather hood over its head. Latharna would be calmer now that she couldn't see.

Dunnottar woods stretched out dark and gloomy for miles around her as Isobel trudged back toward the camp where her father and brother were waiting. Occasional shafts of sunlight broke through the tall canopy of fir, elm, spruce, and oak trees that thrived here.

The majestic falcon rode easily on Isobel's leather glove-covered hand as she walked over tree roots and stone. There was no path to follow, but she remembered going past the forked chestnut tree, so this was the correct direction.

Isobel put down the duck and bent to pick up a few chestnuts from those littering the ground under the tree. She stuffed them in the pockets of the boy's breeches she wore. The nuts would be delicious when roasted. Traveling folks needed to help themselves to food when it became available.

Kak! Kak!

Isobel jerked her head around to look at her falcon. Latharna rarely uttered a peep when she was hooded, and now she had sounded an alarm call.

DIANE WYLIE

The falcon's wings fluttered and she shook herself in a rousing fashion. Something had disturbed the bird.

Isobel froze, listening carefully.

A faint, human cry of distress reached her ears.

It stopped then a few seconds later, she heard it again. Someone needed help. Grahams never turn their backs on someone in need.

Quickly, Isobel stripped the hood off Latharna, released the jesses, and jerked her arm upward. The falcon lifted from her hand and soared up into the sky.

"I'll call ye back later, lassie," she told the departing bird.

Then she hung her duck from a branch by tying its legs with a leather thong.

Finally, Isobel retrieved her *sgian dubh* from the sheath at her belt. Now armed with her knife, she set off in the direction of the noise.

The Scottish Falconers, Book Two: Hunted available soon.

Acknowledgments

Thanks to:

Jack Hubley, a naturalist, who gave me the opportunity to hold a falcon and bring it back to the glove during "The Falconry Experience" in Hershey, PA. He patiently answered all of my questions and provided most of the information about falconry contained in this book.
http://www.jackhubley.com.

Diane and the Falcon

Additional Titles by Diane Wylie

Outlaw Lover

Magic at the Roxy

Magic of the Pentacle

Moonlight and Illusions

Prelude to Magic

Secrets and Sacrifices

Jenny's Passion

Lila's Vow

Adam's Treasure

A Soldier to Love (short story)

Outlaw Lover
by Diane Wylie

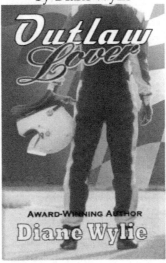

Genre: Romantic Suspense

When Meghan Somerset moves to a small town in Pennsylvania all she wants is to build a new life and put her past behind her. In a stroke of fate, she is drawn to a man whose ambitions embody her worst nightmare—he is an outlaw racer.

Kevin Richards, the son of a farming family, is a weekend sprint car driver whose greatest desire is to become a professional auto racer. But all of the cards seem stacked against him when a string of suspicious accidents threaten his life and the lives of everyone around him.

Magic at the Roxy
by Diane Wylie

Genre: Fantasy/Paranormal Romance

Celeste Macallister is not having a good year. She's been jilted at the altar and laid off from her job. The one, slightly tarnished, bright spot is the old art deco theater in Scotland, The Roxy, left to her by her Aunt Nora. On the advice of her old friend, Harry Cameron, she decides to hire Matthew Stewart, the famous stage magician, to keep the theater alive. It's a good idea…at first.

One minute she's in the 21st century, and the next, Celeste finds herself in a time when The Roxy is new, Harry Cameron is young, and Nazi bombs are raining down on Scotland. It doesn't take her long to figure out it is all Matthew Stewart's fault. To think, she was really beginning to like the man…

Magic of the Pentacle
by Diane Wylie

Genre: Fantasy/Paranormal Romance

As a psychiatrist, Dr. Juliana Nelson deals with her patients' real and imagined problems every day. But the secrets revealed by magician Richard Blackstone, have Juliana questioning her judgment and losing her heart.

Richard's playboy lifestyle suited him for hundreds of years…until he meets Juliana. He tries to hide the power of his five-pointed star amulet, the *Pentacle,* from her until events spin out of control. Now he must face the truth of his past and fulfill the five virtues of a knight of the Order of the Garter or risk losing Juliana for good.

Moonlight and Illusions
by Diane Wylie

Genre: Paranormal Romance

Illusionist Stephen Elliott performs dazzling magic feats to crowded theaters around the world. Then a chance encounter with an old woman and a cursed relic send his perfect life spinning out of control. He ends up cursed, on the run, and...immortal.

From her seat in the twenty-second row, Anabel Bernier recognizes with a jolt the handsome star of the magic show. World War II and the passage of time did nothing to dim the burning memory of her moonlight encounter with the charming Stephen Elliott. Will unexplained events, secrets, and powerful magic threaten their second chance at a future together?

BESIEGED

Lila's Vow
by Diane Wylie

Genre: Historical Romance

Schoolteacher Lila Sutton finds her one true love when cavalryman Captain Jack Montgomery rides into Gettysburg. But receiving word of his death leads her to seek her own type of revenge.

Imprisoned for a year, Jack returns to an uncertain future filled with turmoil and danger, when all he wants is Lila.

Jenny's Passion
by Diane Wylie

Genre: Historical Romance

David Reynolds joined the cavalry out of a sense of duty and adventure. As he rides into battle at Mine Run he has no idea his life is about to change forever.

The forbidden Yankee attracts Jennifer Winston like no other. She would do anything to save him…even kill.

Secrets and Sacrifices
by Diane Wylie

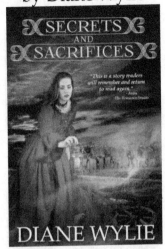

Genre: Historical Romance

The Confederate army is starving and badly in need of clothing. Add to that the mounting numbers of battle casualties, a lack of medical supplies, and army surgeon, Captain Daniel Reid, of the Twenty-Fifth Virginia, knows he has to take action, no matter the consequences.

Charlotte Garrett loses her husband and her identity when she takes on the guise of a Southern soldier. Learning to march, fight, and even spit like a man is to be expected. But what she doesn't expect to find is a situation that leads her into the arms of a new man and into big, big trouble with the North and South!

DIANE WYLIE

Adam's Treasure
by Diane Wylie

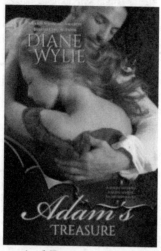

Genre: Historical Romance

Master of disguise, Adam Skelding, is a
Pinkerton agent on assignment. His mission:
Find the missing gold and stop the secretive
Knights of the Golden Circle before they gain
power. The future of the country depends
upon it.

All Marilla Logan wanted was a way to
escape from her life as a tavern wench. A
dark stranger who breaks into her room offers
her only chance. Swept up into a life of
intrigue, she becomes ensnared in a tangled
web of clues, danger, and emotion to break
the code.

About the Author

Author, Diane Wylie, loves books that will take her on an emotional roller coaster ride. What better genre than romance to do that? She has always particularly loved romances with dashing heroes and beautiful heroines.

Diane, a graduate of Rutgers University, had wanted to be either a veterinarian or a marine biologist, but still manages to fulfill her love for science as a technical writer.

The mother of two grown children and grandmother to two cuties, Diane makes her home in Maryland with her husband, Ed and two sassy Pembroke Welsh corgis.

Visit Diane's website: http://www.dianewylie.com to learn more about her and her upcoming novels.

DIANE WYLIE

Made in the USA
Middletown, DE
11 November 2024

64312401R00096